CHRISTMAS KILLS

CLAIRE DAVON   MARK CASSELL   N. J. EMBER
RYAN COLLEY   LILY LUCHESI   AMIR LANE
CHARLES REIS   JON TOBEY
I. CLAYTON REYNOLDS   DALE DRAKE
KEVIN J. KENNEDY

Illustrated by
DEAN SAMED

FRACTURED **Mind**
PUBLISHING

CONTENTS

INTRODUCTION

"Night is not something to endure until dawn. It is an element, like wind or fire. Darkness is its own kingdom; it moves to its own laws, and many living things dwell in it."

Patricia A. McKillip

Make Christmas horror an event again with these delightful tales of holiday treachery. While you're certain to meet some resistance in asking your family to gather around for a yuletide horror tale, give it a shot. It may be just the gift they didn't know they needed.

CHRISTMAS KILLS

A CHRISTMAS HORROR ANTHOLOGY

Here comes Santa Claus,
Bringing you Santa Claus pain.
Vicious old bastard
with sharp-hoofed reindeer
pullin' on the reins.

Bells are ringing,
children screaming,
all is scary with blight.
Say your prayers
or feel your fear,
cuz Santa Claus comes tonight

1

THE YULE TIDE

CLAIRE DAVON

*S*now eddied around Nellie, cloaking her in a world of white.

She stared at the car she left, wondering if it had been a good idea to hoof it. There was no sign of habitation on this rural country road. The storm had come out of nowhere. But that was New England for you. "If you don't like the weather, wait a minute," Nellie muttered as she pulled her coat tighter. Her hands reached for a scarf that was not there. With a sigh, she checked her cell phone, but it showed no signal. She had not been able to get a call or a text for the last five miles. In the end her options narrowed down to one—try and find refuge. It was either that or freeze to death in the useless car that died on her. It had been fine a few hours ago. Then again, she hadn't had a chance to check it out before she roared away from the suburban driveway. Beggars—or robbers— couldn't be choosers. The middle of the lane was still visible, making it easier for her to walk. Better to try and find shelter before the snow accumulated more.

"Awoo!"

The howl pierced the air, making Nellie jump. It sounded like a dog, or more likely a wolf. She fingered the .45 hidden in her stolen parka, the metal cold even through her driving gloves. It made her feel more secure that she had it—that, and the three magazines in her coat pocket.

"Come at me and regret it, wolf."

Her breath came out in white puffs, cold icing her nose. Nellie tugged the ski mask down and pulled her parka hood tighter.

The howl started again, long and piercing. The hairs went up on the back of her neck. A rattling sound accompanied it, and a bell. That made no sense. Her mind had to be playing tricks on her.

Dear old daddy-o wasn't expecting her to turn up in this ass end of nowhere, Massachusetts yet. Her release date had been in January, but she'd gotten out ahead of schedule. Christmas spirit, and all that. Religious fools.

She considered retracing her route and returning to the car. It provided shelter from the wind that picked up and died down at random, bringing swirling drifts with it. She was alone in the elements where folks froze to death. If it had still been running, she might have. She was an idiot to try this journey in early December, but she believed she had the weather on her side.

"Awoo!"

It was impossible to determine where the cry came from. It could be half a mile away, or a handful of feet.

"Fuck off, wolf, or whatever you are. I'm just trying to get to town." When she peered toward where she ca me from, her car was gone. She didn't think she'd gone more than fifty yards, but she lost track of time as well as distance. She rubbed her hands together to create heat and friction. She could find somewhere safe. It was better than waiting for help that might never come. She'd take her chances on the road.

Rattling chains accompanied the howl. She wondered if it was a dog who had gotten away from its lead, but took a piece with him.

When the wail came again, she thought she detected words of pain and loss buried in the noise. She staggered to a halt.

She'd heard that sound before when she'd been locked inside the jail. She almost fancied she could hear people whispering to her there. Some inmates tried that trick and murmured threatening words as she passed. They learned that Nellie was no pushover. The howl then was like it was now, full of longing and desperation—and menace. The sound that early December night kept Nellie up, her attention focused on the sliver of moonlight through her window bars.

When it was light the next morning, Nellie told herself that she had been imagining the desperate cries. It couldn't be a wolf—they didn't get into the cities. More likely it was the common urban coyote searching for prey. Not some wolf hunting for something—for her. Even if it had been a wolf, it wasn't looking specifically for Nellie. The rest of it—the chains, bells, and a whip-crack that accompanied the howl, had been her imagination.

Nothing happened on subsequent nights. No more howls, chains or bells. Over time, she forgot about it. Then, as December drew near, she started to have restless visions again. During the day, she convinced herself she was hallucinating. If her sleep was broken at night, well, that wasn't unusual. Some would call it a guilty conscience, but she never slept well. She continued to make her plans and didn't let some crazy dreams about a baying creature stop her. If it reminded her of that *Twilight Zone* episode where the howling man turned out to be the devil, that was her overactive imagination.

She mostly succeeded in convincing herself of that until tonight, when she heard the same sounds echoing through the forest. If they had been terrifying within the jail, they were twice as scary here. She fingered the gun again. The family she'd taken her supplies from might live. It was hard to say. She couldn't concern herself with that. She'd needed them to get to her father. He wouldn't ignore her when she turned up. Bad seed. Like mother, like daughter. Former mother. What did you call someone who was dead? Ex-mother?

"Awooo...."

She whirled. Her heart was hammering in her chest and a panicked part of her sought to fire into the darkness. The sound of chains and bells rang through the air, as though the animal dragged heavy links across the ground. If someone chained up a beast, they wouldn't put tinkling bells on it. They'd kill it. As she would now.

The pistol was cold in her gloved hand, her finger too thick for the hole of the trigger. She slipped off the glove, tucking her hand with the gun back into the pocket. Even through the parka, she felt the chill on her naked skin.

"Awooo…"

There was something desperately human in that cry. Like that *Twilight Zone* episode. It echoed around her and through her. A bone deep fear seared her soul. She was in the middle of a road, snow drenched , pursued by a wolf.

Fuck it. Time to go back. It had been a mistake to leave the shelter of the auto in the first place. She wasn't getting anywhere in this weather. At least there she had protection if the wolf attacked. All she had to do was and find her way back. It made more sense than staying in the storm. All that was out here was death.

Nellie began heading back in the direction she'd come from. She was almost sure this was the right way. She wished she could make out lights, or smoke—any sign of human habitation. It was too easy to imagine she was alone in the wilderness, out here with…whatever it was.

Her cell rang and she jumped. She reached for it but the music stopped before she could answer. "Missed Call" was all it said. It could be anyone. It might be her father, warning her against showing up—if he'd learned of her release. His last words echoed through her mind: *you're not wanted here. Not ever again. Not after what you did.* They may not have been able to prove her involvement in what happened to her mother, but he knew.

"Awoo…"

The dragging sound was closer.

She fumbled with the phone. She had to get help. Maybe she was far enough away that emergency services here wouldn't connect her with the incident in New Hampshire. She could no longer see the road ahead. As she watched, the cell blinked back to her screen saver, showing a failed sent call on the screen.

"Awoo..."

"Fuck you!" She screamed the words into the night. She looked for movement, a tuft of fur, anything that would indicate what she was facing. "Leave me alone. Just leave me alone."

Her foot caught on something. Nellie stumbled but didn't lose her balance. Precipitation caught on her eyelashes and stuck before melting from her body heat. She stuffed the useless phone in her pocket and then slid her hand back around the gun.

"Awoo..."

Nellie glanced up to make sure that the trees were still on either side of the road. To her relief, she hadn't stumbled off. Her boots were sturdy, but a size too big. Her feet were starting to get numb, the socks she'd stolen inadequate against the piercing cold. She'd been many times a fool to leave the vehicle. The snowstorm wasn't letting up. It might never let up.

Maybe the car was right in front of her and she couldn't see it in the dense storm. She might pass it and not be aware.

"Awoo..."

The noise appeared closer this time, the rattle and clank of chains louder. Nellie wanted to dash screaming into the darkness, but the part of her that was still rational understood she would be dead in a few steps if she gave in to panic. The one hope she had was her intelligence and cunning. Whatever this was, it was just an animal, and she was smarter than any wolf. She could get through this.

"Show yourself, you bastard!" She waved the cold gun in the air, ignoring the chill on her ungloved hand.

Silence fell, as thick as the flakes that still descended . She brushed them out of her eyes, feeling each one mark her skin. She couldn't give in to terror. That was a ticket to disaster.

"Wherever you are, you goddamn wolf, come and get me. I dare you." Nellie took a step back and something crunched under her feet. She'd reached the edge of the road. The trees stood tall and menacing behind her. Something glowed in the distance and she fired one wild shot toward it. For a moment, a burning red stare appeared to focus on her.

Nellie scanned again for her automobile, praying she would get lucky. She tried to peer into the woods, but all she saw was flurries and the blurry outline of tree trunks. The thick blanket of white would be pretty if she were observing it from a window with a cup of hot chocolate and a warm fire in the hearth. Not when the tip of her nose was numb and she could no longer feel her toes. Not when her panicked breath came out in white puffs, visible in the bright moon that showed her surroundings.

She had to stay calm or she was going to pass out. Taking several breaths, Nellie focused on what the stupid relaxation tapes the prison library had recommended. Breathe in on the count of one, two, three, four, and then hold. Release five, four, three, two, one.

Breathe in…

The sound of clanking chains and tinkling bells was loud, echoing through the landscape. Nellie's heart started hammering in her chest and fear sweat broke out along her hairline. She pivoted, peering around for the brute. She might be going crazy. Perhaps she was lying in the bank, her life ebbing away. This might be a death induced hallucination. If it was the afterlife, she was fucked.

Nellie held her gloved hand in front of her and it disappeared into the blizzard. That was impossible. No fall could be that thick. She stuck both hands back into her pockets, with her naked finger still on the trigger.

"Did you think nobody would know? Did you think nobody was aware?"

The syllables were rough, the words slurred as though they came from a person with a speech impediment. She fired a shot in the direction of the voice, despite her admonition not to waste shots. Nellie would have fled, if there had been anywhere to run to. But it was just her in this desolate place where nothing was real but the storm and her phantasm. It had to be some sort of fever dream. The words were weird, wrong, like the speaker had...a mouth full of teeth. Or fangs.

"Where are you? Who are you?"

It was December 5th, a day that was nothing special. She meant to surprise her father—instead she was the one being amazed. If she—when she—got out of this, she'd turn around and flee to New Hampshire. Maybe if she holed up, they'd never link the robbery, and possible murder, to her.

The twin sound of clanking chains and tinkling bells came closer. "Americans, they are so ignorant," the sibilant voice said. It was all around her, in the trees and the snow, the tones filling her ears. She wanted to put her hands up to block out the sound and shriek. But if she started screaming, she might never stop.

"Americans?" She was in New England, the definition of America. "You aren't making sense." Maybe it was some sort of escaped prisoner. The nearest jail was some rinky dink thing in Nashua. The bigger prisons were in larger cities like Manchester, like the one she'd come from. Maybe he was a mental patient. It was likely some crazy wacko who draped himself in chains, high on meth. That would explain why he didn't feel the cold.

"You Americans, you don't have a sense of history."

Her hand trembled, her fingertips icy. She longed to get off another round but couldn't waste the bullets. She supposed there were four more in the chamber, but had lost count. She didn't think she could fire with her fingers so numb.

"Who are you?" The fact that he was talking meant he wasn't a wolf. He might think he was, if he was an escaped mental patient. People believed a variety of weird shit.

Like those who assumed she was worth saving.

The creature that came out of the trees was a thing out of a nightmare. The storm cleared as he approached, enough for her to make out all of him. The man, or thing, stood close to seven feet tall. He wasn't wearing a parka, or clothes, covered instead from head to toe in dark brown fur. His legs were like that of a goat, bending the wrong way. She stared at the hooves that appeared too small to be some sort of footwear. Chains draped around his neck and body, decorated with bells. There was a sack strapped to his back, with something inside wriggling to get free.

The horns that stood out from his head were curved like a goat and tapered to sharp tips. Costume or not, those could cause serious damage. The fear-induced sweat that had dried bloomed again. His tongue flicked out. It was too long for anyone's body—not even Gene Simmons could compete. Now she was sure she was dying in a snowbank after all.

If she was, she would take this…thing…with her.

She pointed the firearm toward the beast.

"Don't come any closer." Nellie's voice shook and she tried to swallow but had no saliva. Chills wracked her body. She would be dead if she didn't get back to the car, to shelter.

The thing moved his tongue around. There was a cry from whatever was on his back. Maybe it was a raccoon, or a cat, something for the crazy man to cook up for dinner.

"You Americans. So foolish. You should have listened to the old folk tales when your father told them, Nellie. If you had, you would have known better than to venture out this night. Bad children are taken on Krampusnacht."

He had an accent that she couldn't place. German, perhaps, or something Eastern European. Maybe he'd immigrated here not too long ago. This might be some batshit crazy tradition from the old country.

"You're nuts." She waved the gun at him. "What the fuck is Krampusnacht? If it's some ritual wherever the hell it is you're from, rest assured it isn't here."

He tsked and waggled a finger at her. "You would have been wise to spend your time in that prison studying history. You knew—somewhere—what I was. You refused to accept it. That was foolish."

She started to laugh, the weapon wavering in her hand.

"Wait a minute. Dad told me something, mostly when he was drunk. He loved those crazy European folk tales. Yeah and there was that stupid horror film Marlon took me to —*Krampus*. You're supposed to be him, aren't you? Dressed up like that fucking German demon? Like you're fooling anyone, you batshit cos player. Give it a rest and get lost."

The chains rattled and the bells rang in the night. The storm stopped, although visibility was still poor. She was shivering, the persistent blizzard chilling her to the core. She had to get somewhere warm. Now.

"Today is December 5th, Nellie. It is the day before the Feast of Saint Nicholas. This is my night. You may not believe in Krampus, but I do not need you to believe. I have all I require from your actions. I've waited a year to do what needs to be done. Come, Nellie. Come to me of your own free will and it will go easier for you."

"Fuck you." She fired a shot at him. It struck him in the torso and pierced the fur and skin in an explosion of brown. Satisfaction filled Nellie at the point-blank shot. No crazy man was going to scare her. Then he shook his shaggy body and straightened. She peered at him, but there was no visible mark where the bullet entered. He chuckled, his tongue sweeping across his cheeks in broad strokes. There was a louder sound from the sack on his back. A head shaped portion stuck from behind his back, and then withdrew into the sack again.

"Thank you, Nellie. It is good to be free of any pretense. Awoo…"

She watched as he lifted his head with those frightening

horns and let loose his utterance into the sky. He finished his cry and turned to her.

"What...are you? If this is some sort of cosplay crap, you picked a hell of a time to do improv." Her body was trembling and she fought to keep the shaking out of her voice.

If a scary demon goat monster could be said to smile, this creature did. He flexed his body and the chains moved with him—as though they were part of him and not constricting. The bells tinkled in what would have been a pleasant sound under different circumstances. Not here. Not now.

"Oh, Nellie, Nellie, don't you wonder how I know your name? I realize that you Americans don't accept the legends of the old country, but I am glad your father told tales of me. You should recall the one of Krampus who comes the night before St. Nicholas and takes away bad children. One night is all that is granted to me, but I make it a good one. You should have heeded your father. Then again, if you had followed your parents, we wouldn't be out here." He reached out his hand. "Come now. It is time for your reckoning. I will make it painless if you cooperate."

The snow thickened, creating a blanket so dense she couldn't see three inches in front of her. The goat man vanished in the fall.

"Yeah, D ad told me those tales, but they were crap then and they're crap now." Her voice shook as she spoke to nobody. She wasn't fooling anyone except herself. In the gale, she wished she'd paid attention to D ad's old stories. Too late now.

Her hand was so cold it was like ice. She struggled to cover her now frozen hand but her other hand was thick and useless inside the glove. She fired; the fear of wasting bullets forgotten. Shots reverberated in the night until the chamber clicked empty. She shoved the firearm back in her coat and turned to run. It no longer mattered where she went. As long as it was away from this crazy Krampus thing.

One step, then two. Panic surged, a fluttering thing that beat inside her body and made her skin tight. Three steps, four.

A chain clinked loud in her ears right before a hair-covered hand fell on her shoulder. Nellie didn't have time to shriek before claws pierced her. She jerked her elbow back. It struck the beast but all he did was laugh. The sound was more terrifying than the howling, because it was human.

"Let me go!" She kicked at the road as she lost purchase with the ground. She twisted in his grip but all that did was make his talons sink in deeper. Blood welled from the wounds and the pain raced through her a moment before the cold kissed her bare skin. The area went numb. It joined her hand, feet and her nose in losing all feeling.

"You deserve special attention, Nellie mine. We honor our parents where I am from." He spun her around to face him, his nails leaving torn cloth and flesh in their wake. The snow lightened around them. Outside their bubble it was as thick as before. They were alone in a frigid hellscape.

"It's not too late. I can change."

He waved a long finger in front of her. Mesmerized, Nellie followed his hand. She no longer wondered where the light came from, or how the snow fell. It was him. Krampus.

"It was too late for change years ago, my dear lost soul. You are mine."

One glance into his eyes, flashing between red and black, told her there was no hope. "I didn't mean…" She hiccupped and flakes slid down her throat. The cold should have burned but it didn't. Her gorge, like the rest of her, was deadened.

"People often don't intend what they do. Yet they must face the consequences."

She swayed in his grip, fatigue filling her.

"I…" Whatever she'd been about to say died on her lips. She gazed up at him and perceived an odd sort of compassion. She couldn't feel her body. "I'm sorry."

"Yes. Yes, you are."

His hands hauled her up by the nape of the neck like a cat would a kitten. There was a brief, searing pain as a claw raked her back, severing her spine. She went limp and he shoved her into the sack that wriggled and twisted with others like her. She took a strange comfort in the fact that at the end, there would be a reckoning. It was what was always going to happen.

When darkness descended, Nellie knew nothing more.

THE END

2

HO HO HOLLOW

MARK CASSELL

"Mum," Kitt said from behind her, "I've got a stomach ache."

Rachel peered over a shoulder.

From her chair at the dining room table, she saw her son looking at her. Lanky for a ten-year- old, he stood framed in the doorway with sleeves halfway up his skinny forearms. Perhaps they should've bought him a new coat rather than all those presents. A glance into the lounge reminded her of the mess to clear up: wrapping paper and toys everywhere. Her and James's gifts were neatly stacked beside the sofa from which they'd earlier watched the chaos unfold.

"You're dripping snow on the carpet," she told him. "Take off your coat."

His face, rosy from the cold, didn't change as he slunk back into the kitchen. The sound of his shuffling feet was almost in time with James's vegetable chopping.

"At least you took off your boots," she called after him.

Coloured Lego bricks of varying shapes and sizes covered the table, several obscuring the instruction booklet and surrounding the half-complete model. Indeed, much like the toys scattered in the other room, this was another present he'd played with for not even five minutes. Most, after tearing open the wrapping paper, he'd simply given a once-over; some, barely a cursory glance. Every year, it was the same. Flo seemed to be following in his ways. As it was, she often copied him, a trait Rachel knew was common in all younger siblings.

She found the Lego brick she'd been searching for, attached it to the part Kitt had already completed, and glanced at the photo on the box. What she had so far in her hands, she guessed, would be a section of car engine. She recalled the 70s, when Lego models were basic vehicles. But now, they were impressive, intricate, and with so many moving parts. Back then, it was pretty much only the wheels that moved. As a kid, she marvelled at how her older brother would construct them. She wondered if she had copied him as much as Flo copied Kitt.

In a few hours, her brother and his children would come crashing through their front door, presents in hand... more chaos... more wrapping paper to tidy later. And, besides... all that packaging – seriously, was all that packaging necessary?

Tea. She wanted a cup of tea, but as she stepped into the kitchen, the smell of brandy and cinnamon warmed her nostrils. When she saw the saucepan of mulled wine steaming on the stove, she knew she had no intention of putting the kettle on to make a cuppa.

Yeah, she wanted some mulled wine.

James didn't look 'round as he said, "I'm looking forward to this."

He dragged a bunch of carrots across the work surface, and with nimble fingers, he began chopping them into even slices. She often marvelled at how he never cut himself. He was a fine cook – indeed, modesty aside, she wasn't too bad herself – and he seemed to enjoy it more than she did.

"Kitt…" He still hadn't removed his jacket. "Where's your sister?"

"Out in the Hollow."

The Hollow, as they'd named it after moving to their country house during the summer, was a bomb crater in the woodland which backed onto their garden. It was one of many overgrown scars from the Second World War. Rachel had once been trapped in a conversation with a local elderly woman who insisted some German pilots hadn't wanted to reach London and so deliberately dropped their payloads onto empty countryside. She was unsure how much faith to have in the woman's knowledge, but it was admirable to be positive about a piece of history that was otherwise devastating.

Positivity, however, was at a low level in Rachel's reserve and she was, sadly, dreading her brother's troops invading her home.

She placed the red Lego brick she hadn't realised she still held onto the worktop. "Why don't you both come in now?"

"I'm in," Kitt said. He unzipped his coat and was now rubbing his stomach.

"Yes, but your sister's not." She reached up and opened

the cupboard for some glasses. "Besides, your cousins'll be here soon."

"I don't feel well." In truth, the boy didn't look himself. Maybe he'd caught a chill. After all, it was cold out there: the sky was white, and the snow was coming down in impressive flurries. However, ever since he'd turned ten he'd become a bit of a whinge-bag.

"Okay." She took two glasses from the shelf and placed them down on the counter. "I'll make some hot chocolate while you go get Flo, and by the time you're back, it'll be ready to drink."

James glanced at her. "Mulled wine for me." He looked at the glasses in front of her and grinned. "Good call."

She watched Kitt continue to rub his stomach. Perhaps he really was ill. "What do you say, sweetie?"

He shrugged.

"Deal?" she prodded.

His eyes drifted from her, to the window and beyond, to where his sister was probably still playing in the den.

"Seriously, Kitt, go get your—"

His face slackened, a whiteness – no, a *blueness* – tinted his cheeks. Traceries of veins raced beneath his skin. His eyes, the whites themselves, turned a cold blue. Ice formed across his cheeks, crackling, and spreading fast to cover his whole face. Even his hair frosted. Clothes, too: they whitened as though he'd been stuffed in a freezer for days.

The sound of crackling intensified.

Rachel staggered forwards, knocking the Lego brick onto the floor. It skittered across the tiles.

James had now turned, eyes wide, knuckles whitening as they gripped the knife.

"Kitt..." she whispered.

His body stiffened. More crackling, sharp, from inside his body, like fracturing ice. His skin, his hands, his face, white as the sky, cracked in places. A deep crevice zigzagged upwards from beneath his collar, shooting along his jaw and up his cheek and across his brow.

He stood there. Frozen.

Fragile as glass, he shattered. Exploded.

Hundreds of multi-coloured ice crystals, twinkling in the kitchen light, shot in every direction. It sounded like a dozen windows cracking at once. In whites and crimsons and purples and blues, their son's body vanished in an icy haze. It was like a bomb had gone off in the middle of an iceberg. Several shards stung Rachel's cheeks.

Her scream filled the kitchen as Kitt became nothing more than hundreds of ice crystals scattered around the kitchen.

Still clutching the knife, James backed off, retched, and spewed. It spattered the worktop, and as it dribbled down the apron she'd bought him for Christmas, she noticed she'd not removed the price tag.

A hundred thoughts collided in her suddenly small brain. Dizziness pressed down on her. What was left of Kitt absurdly made her think of the time she'd dropped the ice cube tray and the cubes had scattered across the tiles.

James stepped forward and reached out for where Kitt had stood. He then backed up... his foot shot out in front of him. Vomit flicked in the air, and for a crazy second, it was as though he ran on the spot.

He fell – face down – onto the knife he still held.

Blood pumped from his chest as he scrambled sideways, then slumped, and kicked the glinting ice crystals. They made the same sound as the Lego brick a moment ago.

"James!" She leapt towards him and dropped to her knees beside his shuddering body.

His moans, strong at first, weakened… softening, quietening. He jerked and a slice of carrot shot across the floor, bounced off a crystal, and skidded through a small heap of snow to rest against one of Kitt's boots. One more twitch, another… then he stopped. His head flopped to the side.

She pulled him into her arms, stroking his face. His dead eyes stared past her head. A dark pool soaked her trousers, warm, now spreading beneath them both. She screamed and her agony tore through the house. A glance out through the glass of the back door, into the relentless snow and out to the bottom of their garden, she remembered Flo. The Hollow.

Tears prick ed her eyes as much as darkness crept into her periphery. Somehow… somehow she pushed both aside.

Flo. She had to get Flo.

* * *

On her feet, not realising she'd stood, she glanced down at James. His blood had now spread to blend in with the crystals that had once been their son. With one boot on, one off, she reached for the backdoor, gripping it with slippery fingers.

James couldn't be dead, could he? Can't be possible. And Kitt. What happened to Kitt? She staggered back towards her husband, refusing to believe any of this. The sole of her Wellington boot squeaked, slipping in the blood, and she stumbled into the dishwasher, causing it to rattle.

Leaving red handprints up the front of the appliance, she put on her boots properly.

Flo.

Back to the door, after fumbling the handle, she was soon outside, the air freezing her lungs. A quick look over her shoulder brought into view James's legs amid the glinting crystals, and she considered going back to get a coat.

But… the Hollow – she had to get to the Hollow.

Already, Kitt's footprints had vanished.

Snow filled the sky, coming down in flurries. It stung her face as she started to run up the pathway, every footfall crunching. In what felt like hours, she made it to the gate at the bottom of their garden – the one James had purposefully cut into the fence to allow access to the woodland behind, so the kids could play in the Hollow. Acres spread out behind their property, where even the Estate Agents couldn't tell them who owned it. All of it so remote, it was never to be a problem.

Something red flashed up ahead, someone darting between tree trunks and winter-dead foliage… then nothing. Perhaps she hadn't seen anyone. But, then again, no... she *knew* she saw him – yet it was ridiculous *who* she saw. This wasn't happening! And it was at that moment, despite the freezing snow buffeting her, she knew she was dreaming… she had to be… surely.

Father Christmas. Or at least someone dressed like him.

A sickness rose in her throat... James, Kitt. Dear God, what was happening? She bit down on her lip and fought the urge to collapse to her knees, to cry, to let the snow take her, freeze her. She remained upright, managing to sprint into the woodland. The snow on the ground thinned the deeper into the woods she went. As she ran, she searched for Father Christmas – for Santa... for the man she'd seen... This was such madness. Kitt had... had exploded! Whatever the cause, she wondered if that man in the red suit had anything to do with it. Kitt had said he felt ill. Poison? Had the imitation Father Christmas poisoned him? Insane. The man—

Rachel interrupted her own thoughts. Flo! He'd better not harm her.

With those thoughts, she sprinted through crispy leaves and snow, kicking it up. Already, she felt damp through her trousers, and James's blood was freezing her skin. The trees were sparser here, and so the snow was thicker, in the sky as well as on the ground. Finally, she saw where the woodland floor dipped slightly. That was where the crater began – the Hollow.

Where had the man gone? There were no footprints. She could've sworn he ran this way. It was snowing heavily, certainly, but not enough to cover his tracks that quickly. Everywhere was a mix of white and subtle streaks of brown where tree trunks and foliage had so far avoided the heavy snow. Her breath clouded the air in front of her and she regretted not getting a coat.

She held up an arm as a feeble shield from the stinging snow.

At the rim of the Hollow, her breath cold and sharp in her throat, she looked down. Below her, in the centre of the crater, was the kids' den. In the shape of something between a cabin and a teepee, built with James's carpentry skills, it was a sturdy weave of branches and pallet boards. Snow covered the roof and heaped the sides in drifts.

Still, she saw no sign of Father Christmas.

A short laugh escaped her, and she refused another as it seemed to get lost in the snow. She worried that would bring on a madness she felt was close to overwhelming her, like the darkness she felt at the edge of her vision. She stumbled down the slope, almost tripping, but snagged herself on the winter skeleton of a tree. Beside her, a startled redbreast robin took flight. The branch it had been standing on wobbled in the wake of its lift-off.

Flo *had* to be down there… she hoped… she prayed.

Down the embankment she went, taking sideways steps between branches and tangled brambles. The snow was untouched here, too. Again, she wondered about the man she'd seen. *Had* she seen him? Whoever he was, and indeed if she'd even seen him, couldn't be in the den. No footprints, she thought with relief.

But she knew her daughter was in there. She couldn't be anywhere else.

Rachel slowed her pace, her lungs burning with a strange, cold fire, and her breath plumed about her in great clouds.

"Flo?" Her voice sounded close to hysterical, and, again, she somehow pushed it aside. She reached the paving that hid beneath the smooth snow. "Honey?"

No answer.

Closer to the door, she saw colours between the snow-coated boards and branches; bright yellow, too. Was that Flo's coat? Yes, thank God. There she was, sitting inside.

"It's Mummy, I'm coming in." Rachel pulled open the door, and it made an arc in the snow. "Flo, honey…"

Her daughter sat cross-legged on the blanket the kids used as a carpet. For a moment, Rachel couldn't understand what she saw. Food. So many paper plates, piled with food, surrounded her daughter. She wondered at which point during the day her children had taken all the food from the kitchen. Had it been today? Yesterday? Then Rachel realised none of the food was theirs. She didn't recognise any of it. There was a Christmas pudding and gingerbread men, mince pies, iced biscuits, tree cookies, and a perfectly-made Yule log. The chocolate looked *divine*.

Flo turned towards her. There was a headless gingerbread man in her pudgy fingers, and through a mouthful, she said, "Mummy, I told Kitt not to eat it."

A flash of memory: Kitt rubbing his stomach, turning to ice, exploding… She wanted to laugh, to cry, to tell Flo to stop eating, and… she wanted some of that chocolate log. Kitt, James… a shiver ran up her spine, and she crouched to step through the doorway.

She slapped the gingerbread from the girl's hand.

"Don't eat anything!" Tears again threatened to overcome her. She bit her lip, feeling her chin quiver.

Shocked, Flo cradled her hand in the other, and declared, "It tastes fine."

"Kitt—" Her boy's name caught in her throat.

"He shouldn't have eaten any of *that*." Flo pointed to a

plate Rachel hadn't noticed tucked between the Yule log and Christmas pudding. It was a pie with a smiling elf's face made from chunks of lumpy pastry. Crudely made, and entirely unappetising. There was a piece missing, and the filling oozed a deep red onto the plate. It glistened, reflecting Flo's yellow coat.

Again, she thought of Kitt's exploding body. Again, she bit her lip. This was not the time to lose her cool.

Wind howled, and through the gap in the branches and boards, snow drifted in. Several flakes landed on the elf pie to instantly dissolve into the pastry and filling.

Rachel's lip hurt, and the copper taste of blood teased her tongue. Perhaps it even trickled down her chin. A shuffle forwards, and she could finally wrap her arms around Flo. Tight. An embrace. Mother and daughter. A life-thread... Family. Her only family now. Tears welled, blurred her vision. It was like water filled the den, brimming to drown them both. As though that was precisely what was happening, she began to choke and gasp. But they were sobs.

"He's outside again," Flo whispered.

Rachel gulped, held back the next sob, and mumbled into the girl's hair, "Who?"

"I'm scared, M ummy."

With reluctance, she held Flo at arm's length. "Who are you talking about?" Rachel knew. Of course she knew.

Flo's eyes widened.

Outside, the sounds of twigs breaking and snow crunching beneath boots made them squeeze one another tighter.

The air froze in Rachel's throat.

In a roar of snapping wood, exploding splinters and screeching nails, the roof and walls of the den were suddenly ripped away. . A blanket that had been bunched in the corner was swept up into the air. Wind and snow buffeted them, and they both squinted into the whiteness.

Through the swirling snow, the toothy grin of a pock-marked and bearded face bore down on them. The rotund man was dressed in a tatty Father Christmas costume. Frost clung to the grubby fibres. A long, arthritic hand jerked towards Flo, one finger extended. The dirt beneath the finger-nail hovering in front of the girl's nose was black.

"You!" His voice was sharp. "I told you… to… eat!"

Flo's bottom lip quivered.

Rachel shoved her away from him, and stood up straight. Flo cried out amid scattered plates and crumbled food, as Rachel tilted her head back. The man – if she could, in fact, call him that – had to be over eight feet tall. He reeked of a mixture of cinnamon and sewage.

"Who are you?" she shrieked, her hands shaking. Adrenaline buzzed in her head.

When he grinned, his teeth appeared to lengthen, each as sharp as a pine needle and just as green. His red face was cratered, deeply scarred, oozed pus. He wore the floppy, red and white hat of an average Father Christmas, and his bulky coat was of the same shade of red, its buttons tarnished, rusted. A cold, cobalt blue fire burned in his stare – the same coldness that was in Kitt's eyes… just before… before he…

"What have you *done*?" Her shrill voice echoed around the Hollow. Yet again, she realised how close a personal darkness was to taking her away, but she had to stay strong for Flo. It was all about Flo . They had to get out of there – now!

Breath steamed from gaping nostrils as he stepped back, gloating. As he did so, a plate flicked up crumbs over his tatty leather boot and a tree cookie crumbled into the blanket. He shifted the sack she'd not noticed he held. Covered in frost, just like the rest of him, it was crudely stitched in a patchwork effort that was confusing, and not entirely Christmassy. Each section was different: snowmen, love hearts, candy canes, shamrocks, skulls, pumpkins, eggs, rabbits; there was even a baby in a crib. Those were all she glimpsed, but there were more.

A grey-green filth oozed from in between the stitches, dripping onto the ground. It hissed, dissolving the snow and singeing the twigs. It smouldered when it splattered the blanket. An acrid curl of smoke wafted upwards, only to be snatched up by a sudden snow flurry.

"Flo, honey…" Rachel said, fighting the urge to cower before the gruesome creature. "Come here." Her hands shook so much more than from the cold that rooted her.

Flo reached up, and with a cold and clammy grip, grabbed Rachel's hand.

The man's blue eyes, with a hint of red, locked onto Rachel. Unable to look away, she felt Flo yank her sleeve.

"Mummy!"

One more step back, and the fake Father Christmas shrugged off the sack. It slumped to the ground between them with a thump.

"What have I done, you ask?" Incredibly, his grin widened

still, seeming to split his head in two. Those craters in his skin now leaked a greenish muck.

Rachel moved slightly, and a branch snapped beneath her heel. She felt as though the ground had frozen up around her boots.

In one movement, his veiny hands untied the frayed rope that fastened the sack. It gaped for a second then fell sideways. Dozens of coloured crystals scattered... and James's body flopped out.

Her heart corkscrewed into her throat and she cried out.

"Daddy!" Flo's grip crushed Rachel's fingers.

Most of the crystals and the majority of her husband's body remained in the sack. Those icy shards of her son twinkled.

"What have I done, indeed!" He laughed and it was more a shriek of delight, the sick bastard.

Flo pulled against Rachel's hand, but she wouldn't let her rush to her dad. No way.

"And..." The man booted James's lifeless body. "I even have a bonus."

James's dead eyes stared up to the sky as though watching the drifting flakes. A bitterness rose in Rachel's throat, choking her, and her mind reeled and warped her vision.

This man, this *monster*, reached down and picked up one of the crystals. He squinted into it, rolling it between thumb and forefinger. "Beautiful," he muttered and flicked it back into the sack. That tinkling sound sent nausea flushing through her. Still crouched, he picked up the elf pie. Its filling bubbled.

Rachel willed her feet to move, and, finally, they shuffled backwards – inches at a time – slowly dragging Flo with her. As before, a dizziness threatened to take her down.

Balancing the plate on his upturned hand, he stood and offered it to Flo.

"Now, eat!"

She shook her head, clamping her lips tight; they turned as white as her cheeks and her tiny nostrils flared.

"I only need one more of you, then I can leave this ridiculous season."

"Get away from her!" Rachel yelled. One hand squeezed Flo's hand, while the other dug fingernails into her own palm to force away the darkness.

"Only one more mouth to feed, then I am out of here, away from this selfish season of gift-sharing-loveless-family-nonsense."

"One more?" Rachel murmured. The dizziness was strengthening, but she had to get Flo away from there.

"Yes." His eyes shone a deeper red amid the blue.

"Just one more?" she repeated, her voice shaking as much as the rest of her. "Then you'll leave us?"

"Yes." He took the plate away from Flo, and tilted his head to look at Rachel.

She straightened her back, lifting her head high. "I'll eat it," she whispered.

"Mummy, no," Flo cried.

Holding that monster's cold gaze, Rachel hardened her next words.

"If you promise to leave my daughter alone, I'll—"

Without waiting for her to finish, he rammed the pie towards her. His grin seemed to fill her whole vision.

Without hesitation, she snatched the plate from him and brought the pie to her mouth. It tasted of cinnamon, rotten vegetables, and off-meat. She gobbled, chewed, swallowed, then choked. Tears came, and then body-wracking sobs followed along with the image of James, of Kitt, of Flo... of a Christmas morning that began so normal.

She released Flo and used both hands to shovel the foul stuff into her mouth.

The man in the red suit chuckled.

"The more you eat," he whispered, "the quicker it'll be."

Gagging, she managed to swallow more. Some slopped onto her boots. Most of it went down her throat.

"Mummy." Flo had backed away and was almost sitting on the splintered remains of the den. A tiny crease formed in her forehead, and her bottom lip quivered.

Rachel dropped the empty plate. The backs of her hands whitened as they frosted. Her lungs filled with freezing air. Then feeling as though her organs had chilled to burning cold, her stomach swelled. A dizziness swept into her blurred vision, a whiteness leaking into her periphery.

So cold! she thought, numbed. *But no pain...*

As she watched ice crystals form over her sleeve and across her jumper, the freezing sensation intensified. The sound of cracking came from somewhere inside her.

Her skin began to split.

From inside to out, that coldness surged through every inch of her, and perhaps... perhaps she heard Flo call out before a darkness replaced the blinding whiteness… and Rachael shattered into hundreds of ice crystals.

The girl cowered against the splintered remains of the den, her arm covering her face. Wind roared and snow stung her forehead. When she looked around, through a tornado of red and white and multi-coloured ice, she saw the pretend Father Christmas. He flew around her, swooping up and down, circling.

It was like she was trapped in a storm, and it made her dizzy. Her throat hurt from screaming, but she couldn't hear herself over the shrieking wind.

The man's ugly patchwork sack gaped open to scoop the crystals. Soon, the colours dissolved into the whorl of snow, and even his red suit blended with the white. She could barely see him now.

Although the man had vanished, his laughter remained close.

"Better go indoors, little girl…" h is words shrieked, then faded with a dying wind, "or you'll freeze to death."

3

COLD SNAP

N.J. EMBER

*S*omething dies before the end of a relationship. Either the desire, the trust, or the willingness to keep trying. Or maybe it's the forgiveness. But whatever it is, the love always lingers. Why is it that love is always the last to die?

She'd given Jesse plenty of chances. Fought for the relationship. Given warnings and ultimatums. There was no way Jesse was using again. Gwen kept telling herself that as she watched him shiver while he untangled the Christmas lights. It was what she'd been telling herself all day. Just because she wasn't cold didn't necessarily mean it wasn't. Cabins weren't the best at keeping in heat. Were his hands shaking or was it a trick of the light? Her stomach twisted uneasily, and she looked away before he could catch her watching him. Two days before Christmas wasn't the time to bring this up. This trip was about bringing them back together, not widening the rift between them with more fighting.

Gwen settled deeper into the lumpy sofa, trying in vain to make herself more comfortable, and returned to her research paper for her myths and legends course. She skimmed the webpage, hoping it would help her regain her train of thought. She had titled her paper, *Hecate: Greek Goddess of the Crossroads*, but that was as far as she'd gotten. She huffed, rubbing her eyes with the heels of her palms.

"Do you want to talk through it?" Jesse asked as he stood, brushing pine needles and dog hair off his faded Levi s.

The smile he gave her was overly bright and it didn't match the uncertainty in his eyes. *He's trying. Try with him.*

"Am I being that obvious?"

Jesse counted with his fingers. "First, there was the cleaning, then the pacing and now you're sighing. That's the trifecta of Gwen frustration," he said.

"I just don't know how to write this paper without it sounding like I copied it word for word off the internet. I can't focus."

He tipped one of the empty plastic storage containers over and sat down across from her. "So tell me what you know. Maybe something will click."

She pulled up her notes and read. "Hecate or Hekate, spelled with a k, is a goddess in Ancient Greek religion or mythology. In Hesiod, she is the daughter of the Titan Perses and the nymph Asteria and has power over heaven, earth, and sea; hence, she bestows wealth and all the blessings of daily life. She is sometimes depicted in triple form, like the three fates or the furies, and is associated with crossroads, entryways, night, light, witchcraft, ghosts, necromancy and knowledge of herbs and poisonous plants. She is associated with many animals, including black dogs. Black dogs or hellhounds are often depicted at her side, but being a shape shifting goddess, she can transform into a black dog herself.

"Other symbols used with Hecate are torches. She witnessed the abduction of Demeter's daughter Persephone to the underworld and, torch in hand, assisted in the search for her. Thus, pillars called Hecataea stood at crossroads and doorways, perhaps to keep away evil spirits."

Jesse rubbed the back of his neck. "Couldn't you have picked a less creepy goddess to write about?"

She closed the laptop lid a little, pulling it closer to her. "I don't think she's creepy. I think it's fascinating how she's represented across different cultures. How she's interpreted. Plus, she likes dogs. She can't be all bad."

Dax padded over to her as if he'd been summoned by name, his tail wagging furiously and hitting both of them in the shins. His pink tongue lolled out as he placed his front paws on the edge of the sofa and looked over at her. "Finished your sweep of the place? Come on then," Gwen said, patting the cushion next to her.

Their golden retriever leapt up, turning in a circle once before plopping down and resting his head on her knee. Gwen gave him a scratch behind the ears. "I bet she'd love Dax."

"Everybody loves Dax. It doesn't make her less creepy," Jesse said, grumbling.

"Agree to disagree."

"Anyway, it sounds like you have a good start right there. Go off that."

Gwen frowned. "I don't know. It still feels like something is missing."

"You'll figure it out. Why not take a break?"

It felt like taking breaks was the only thing she had accomplished all day, but she wasn't going to argue. Obviously nothing was coming together right now and doing something else was often the best way to unknot her brain.

Gwen looked around the room. Jesse had worked hard decorating the cabin, making it feel like Christmas. Snowflake clings were stuck to the windows, the ceramic snow-topped houses and businesses of her Christmas village were placed on tables wherever they could fit, even their stockings were hung on the wall with temporary hooks. The lights were finally wrapped around the tree they bought, (a real one, because she never had one before) and now he was busy underneath it, laying down plastic tracks for a train set.

"Do you want me to decorate the tree?" she asked.

His reply came out a bit muffled. "I thought we'd decorate it together."

Together. The thought made her heart flutter traitorously. "Yeah, we should."

The toy train's horn blew twice, catching Dax's attention. His ears drew back and he barked as Jesse crawled out from underneath the tree and the train completed a lap around its base. It made chugging noises as it went, horn blowing occasionally. As Gwen watched Jesse's face light up with excitement, she couldn't help thinking he looked like a little boy. Or maybe just more like the happy, unburdened man she'd first fell in love with. The man he'd been before the drugs. The man who loved her.

Suddenly the hole of her loneliness and grief seemed to swallow her up. Because that's what killed her most nights as she stayed up crying, that's what ate at her. For so long she had waited for the person she loved to come back. To come back home to himself. To come home to her.

Because for so long he was a sullen, depressed, angry stranger. One who hated her. And it was hard being a second choice to something that was literally killing him. Every day that she looked at him and he stared right through her, not even seeing her, she shrank a little more. Until she felt like nothing.

She'd almost forgotten how beautiful it was to see him smile at her. Warm tears poured down her cheeks and she couldn't hold back the sob that tore from her throat. She wanted so badly for him not to be using again. She wanted to believe. She reached her arms around and hugged herself.

Dax whined as he nuzzled her face and tried to climb into her lap.

"Baby? Baby, what's wrong?"

Jesse was next to her now, trying to hold her, trying to wipe the tears from her face. "Are you okay?"

It had been so long since he looked at her pain and acknowledged it. How did they get here?

Usually she tiptoed around her feelings. Any little thing could set him off. Even if it was something he did wrong. Like the time he spent all their grocery money for the month.

But right now, she felt safe, and she couldn't think of anything to say but the obvious. Even if it started an argument. So she told the truth.

She hiccuped as she tried to calm herself. "I thought you stopped loving me."

"No, honey, I could never do that."

It was a lie, but she didn't care . It was okay. Right now there was hope. And that was enough to get them through Christmas.

They did end up decorating the tree together. The angel at the top shined like a good omen. By the time Gwen climbed into bed that night, with Jesse at her side and Dax at their feet, she felt more content and closer to him than ever.

But when she woke again at three in the morning, Gwen's feeling of unease returned. Jesse's side of the bed was empty. *It doesn't mean anything.* But experience and Jesse's history made her doubt.

She had a choice. She could go back to sleep or she could go look for Jesse. Curling up with Dax and snuggling under the covers sounded better than facing a cold reality.

"Dax?" Gwen called. She rubbed the sleep from her eyes. The dog wasn't laying at the end of their bed anymore and she couldn't hear him in the room. She didn't know if they were lucky or unlucky to have a dog that snored.

So Gwen got up and used the bathroom. When she had washed her hands and went to open the bathroom door, she noticed her bare feet sticking to the tile. She glanced down and startled. There were red, blurry outlines of her footprints covering the floor. She sat down and inspected the soles of her feet. She couldn't feel any glass or anything else that might've cut them. She also couldn't find any wounds.

Which means she had to have stepped in something. Gwen went into the hallway and checked the floor. It was damp. The hairs on the back of her neck stood up. Something was wrong. *I need my phone. Where did I leave my phone?*

Gwen thought back. She didn't bring it to bed with her. It was dying from her using it all day, so she left it on the charger in the living room. The lights were on in there. She listened, but she couldn't hear anything.

"Dax?" she whispered, hoping that he would come running and reassure her everything was okay. But he didn't.

She crept into the living room. A man was sitting with Jesse on the couch, pressing a gun to his head. "I didn't want it to go like this, but just do as you're told, honey, and we'll all have a merry Christmas."

Jesse screamed as the bone separated. The stranger set the hammer and chisel down, the tip gently dripping blood on the surface of the coffee table. They'd turned the Christmas tree on before they started. Its glow was nostalgic and innocent, contrasting horribly to the sickening scene in front of Gwen. She'd tried to shut her eyes, but the stranger clucked his tongue at her like a father admonishing a child. "Ah aht, eyes open. Look at me."

But there was nothing paternal in the way he said it or the way his eyes roamed over her, and that only added to the ways the stranger unnerved her.

He didn't look or act the way she expected. He was clean, well-groomed, with manicured nails, and well-dressed in an expensive, probably tailored, red suit. He reminded Gwen a little of Harry Hamlin, with his dark, heavy brows and the parenthetical lines framing his mouth. His voice wasn't harsh or demanding. He didn't bark orders at the two men who yanked Jesse off the couch and forced him to his knees. He didn't seem irritated by the way Jesse flailed and thrashed against the goons' hold as they held his forearms to the coffee table. He was calm, almost statuesque, up until the moment Jesse slumped silently in defeat. Then he gave an almost imperceptible smile. He stood, picking up the hammer and chisel, and the look on his face right before he started made her blood run cold.

"Where's my money, Jesse?"

His voice was so low he almost whispered, but his tone was firm. It was like the way he had spoken to Gwen, playfully, but there was an undercurrent of malevolence. This man didn't make statements or threats. He made promises. And he enjoyed every minute of the torture. He enjoyed watching her squirm.

The stranger had broken two of Jesse's fingers so far and she flinched each time. Her legs shook against her zip tie restraints, the plastic biting into her skin, but she wouldn't cry. She wasn't going to give him any more satisfaction. She knew he was waiting for one of them to break, but Gwen wasn't stupid. No one was going to hear them out here.

Gwen wasn't sure who the stranger was, but now she'd guess he was a dealer. Jesse's dealer. Even as terrified as she was, bound and gagged on the floor, resentment radiated through her. She believed in him and the pain of his betrayal came in waves.

"I don't have it, Scopas, I swear," Jesse said. His breathing was labored, his words came out in huffs and his face looked waxy and pale from sweat and blood loss. He avoided looking at her, speaking to his knees instead.

Scopas. Now the stranger had a name. Gwen knew his name. Which meant if she wasn't going to die before, she was now. Criminals didn't let you live once you could identify them. Although he hadn't bothered to hide his face. Which meant they'd been dead already. He was just drawing this out. Savoring it. Dread turned her insides into lead.

Scopas chuckled, locking eyes with her. "Do you know how much money Jesse owes me, Gwen?"

She shivered. It was the first he ever addressed her directly. *How long has he known my name? How long has he been planning this? Has he been watching us?*

Now Jesse looked at her too, eyes wide. Scopas went over to her, standing above her so she was positioned between his legs. When he squatted down to brush her long hair away from her face, she jolted at his touch. "Easy," he said, pulling the gag down and out of her mouth. He was playful again, his voice turning to silk, toying with her. He brushed his hand along the side of her face again, running his fingers down her side this time, too. Gwen forced herself not to move.

"Good girl. If you misbehave the gag goes back in. Do you understand?"

If she was going to die anyway, she didn't want to play along with his games. She didn't answer. He waited. She imagined him stilled over her, like how he sat at the end of the couch, watching Jesse as he struggled. Then, finally, she felt the hem of her nightshirt being inched up.

His breath tickled the back of her neck as he spoke. Each time he paused he inched it up a little more. "You're so beautiful. Like a work of art. But sometimes beautiful things need to be broken in order to be fully appreciated. To be valued to their fullest potential. Do you want me to break you, Gwen? I have the gun. But they're so distasteful. So pedestrian. Do you want to get my chisel? I'll take more time with you than I did with Jesse. Maybe take you back to my workshop. Introduce you to my other tools."

She was still looking towards Jesse, her cheek pressed to the rough wood floor. She could see the moment he snapped. She watched him try to break free. She watched as the other men beat him and forced him back down. She watched him lose.

Scopa's voice was in her ear now. His words only for her. "Twenty thousand dollars, Gwen. Is Jesse worth twenty thousand dollars? I mean, really, look at him. He can't protect you. And did he use any of that money on a wedding or towards a home for the two of you? No. He spent on himself. So, are you going to answer my questions or do I have to get you to open up a different way? I'd love to make some art out of your insides."

She didn't mean for it to happen. The urine flowed down her legs, warm and wet, musty, pooling underneath her. It coated her like a manifestation of her shame. But it didn't faze him. He waited.

"I knew about the drugs. I mean, I thought he might've

been using again. But I didn't know about you or anything about your money," she said.

"It sounds like she's telling the truth, Jesse."

He stepped over her. Left her behind. Now it was Gwen who couldn't look at Jesse.

"She is. Gwen doesn't lie," Jesse replied.

"Gwen doesn't lie. Unlike you. But you'll tell me where my money is, Jesse. The question is, how? You've lost your dog. You've lost the use of three of your fingers. What will it take to make you an honest man?"

"I don't have it. I just don't have it. I swear."

Scopas glanced towards her again. He had that look in his eye. The one she'd seen before he'd started breaking Jesse's fingers. She threw herself backwards, trying to crawl away from him. He smiled as he pulled a white handkerchief from his breast pocket and lazily wiped the chisel clean.

"No! Please! I can get it. I'll get the money. I swear!"

"Sin always brings in the devil, Jesse. I am the demon you invited to your door. And the devil always gets his due. But it is Christmas, after all. Maybe I can be merciful. Just once."

Gwen kept trying to scoot her way to the door. He wasn't capable of mercy. That much she knew.

"I'll get you your money. Just let Gwen go."

"Are you sure that's what you want, Jesse? Think carefully. Because I'll give you a choice. Either you or Gwen. Pick who gets to live."

Gwen stopped moving. She stared at Jesse. She wanted him to choose her to live, but it wasn't a simple choice. She knew that. Who would willingly choose their own death if given the choice? And if Scopas had given her the same choice, would she have chosen Jesse to live over herself? Did she love him enough to do that? Maybe once, before all this. All the lies, secrets and betrayal. Before the rift formed between them. But now?

She knew what the answer was, but she still wanted him to choose her because it was the last chance he had to do it. She wanted him to put her before himself so she would go knowing all their years together hadn't been meaningless. She wanted to know there was still something left of his love for her. But maybe earlier when they decorated the cabin was all the closure she'd get in this life.

All of her hope dwindled to nothing. She saw the answer in his face too. She wanted to reassure him. To tell him it was okay. But it wasn't really. As she cried it was because she had nothing left to lose. She didn't care anymore.

"Jesse?"

She hadn't meant for his name to come out like a plea or a question, but somehow it sounded like both.

"I'm sorry, Gwen. I love you," Jesse said in a hollow voice.

This time Scopas's men held her down as he stood over her. The chisel and hammer were already in his hands. "I didn't expect anything less from you, Jesse. But at least now everyone here understands what kind of man you are. Now Gwen gets to pay for your lies and your sins."

Gwen felt the chisel pressed firmly against her lower back.

"Too bad. It means she'll have to suffer a terrible ordeal on your behalf. I'm going to puncture both her kidneys. It's a slow, painful way to die. And don't look away, or I'll do you next instead of letting you go and giving you a week to get my money. Do you understand?"

"Oh God. Gwen, I'm so sorry. I'm so sorry, baby. I love you."

"Tell me you understand, Jesse."

"I understand, okay? Just stop."

"Sometimes beautiful things need to be broken in order to be fully appreciated. I'm going to bring her to her fullest potential. To her highest value. She's going to be my masterpiece."

Gwen shut her eyes and tried to brace herself as the hammer swung down.

She could feel herself dying. She could feel the life inside her slipping away with the blood loss even as her heart beat valiantly, trying desperately to cling to life. Do you know the feeling right before anesthesia puts you to sleep during surgery? That floating void in between not really awake but not yet unconscious? There's just a moment of panic, a split second shock in the way we are separated from our skin, reminded that we are liquid against our skeletons, souls untethered by form or gravity.

Dying is a lot like that. A string unwinding as it's cut free. A balloon floating up and away against the clear blue sky.

She thought of fireworks as white flashed against the inky edges of her vision. She wanted to see her life in them, something good and kind to lead her into her final dream, like the way her mom's kiss on the forehead used to do. There's no pain anymore as the lights dim and go out like stars. Only the cold stays. So cold.

"Please don't make me float," she begged to the nothing. "I'm terrified without something to ground me. Something to hold on to."

She knew she was going. She'd split into two. The Gwen dying in the snow- covered ditch and the Gwen watching from above. She was like water flowing back and forth between two containers.

Eventually, she would pour out. "Please."

Her last thought was of Dax. Her sweet puppy hadn't deserved to die either. Her vision pin-holed. Everything faded into night.

The cold and pain faded as warmth surrounded her. It filled her up from the inside out like a shot of whiskey or a warm cup of tea. Wherever she was, she was safe now. Orange light glowed in the distance, growing closer the longer she looked. Eventually, Gwen could make out the form of a giant bear. No. It was a dog.

Dax?

She didn't know if she thought the words or said them out loud, but as it grew closer she knew it couldn't be Dax. This dog was pitch black with a thick, shaggy coat and a bulky frame. It almost resembled a wolf. There were two of them striding on either side of a woman. The woman was clothed in long skirts, or maybe a dress, which shifted around her in colors of black and slate gray. Everything surrounding her seemed to flicker and undulate like storm clouds, shadows, or a dark sea, and she carried two blazing torches in her hands. Something about her prickled at something in Gwen's memory. It was like a name at the tip of her tongue.

Then it came to her. *Hecate.*

The goddess appeared in front of Gwen as if she had called her name. Maybe she had. There were three of her now, each woman reaching out to comfort her while the hounds licked her face and nuzzled her hair. The women embraced her like a mother, gently rocking her as they healed her wounds. The hounds reminded her of Dax and the pain of missing him squeezed her heart. But the pain didn't linger, the goddess absorbed it as she shifted into one singular being, making Gwen whole again, too.

Hecate studied her, almost like she was asking Gwen something, but she didn't understand the question. All she felt now was peace and contentment. The goddess placed her hand on Gwen's chest, her fingers sinking in deeper until she held Gwen's heart. When she pulled it out it shined in her palm like a sunlight ruby and Hecate's eyes glowed white like the moon.

Gwen wasn't afraid. Hecate spoke to her, she told Gwen her names, names of old, names in languages she didn't understand and names that were long since forgotten. *Raven mother.* Gwen liked that one.

Hecate saw all of Gwen's life. At last, Gwen was able to revisit her memories. She saw memories of good times, of people she loved, memories of loss and, finally, memories of great pain. The screams from Gwen's final moments made it too unbearable to watch. She pressed her palms to her ears to block out the sound. Hecate touched her forehead, making her calm again.

Hecate showed her other women. Women whose own cries of pain and sorrow echoed around them. They cried out for help. They cried out for protection. They cried out for justice. For love. For deliverance. For death. Gwen felt her own connection to them through the goddess in a way she never could in life, each life so evanescently human, every pain a burden to be felt and shared. They were her and she was them. How could she ever have felt alone when they all so intertwined?

Will you go back for them?

Gwen didn't want to go back. Living was accepting the suffering as much the joy, the mundane as much as the divine, and she had suffered enough. To be human meant sacrifice and she had given enough. Hecate showed her the women again, let Gwen listen to their prayers and supplications. She showed Gwen their hopes and dreams.

Avenge them. Avenge yourself.

"How?"

Be my blade and I will be your shield. Become the scale. Become the dark and the light.

Hecate kissed Gwen's forehead and she finally understood. She would go back.

And she would make them all pay.

They buried her in a shallow grave on the side of the road. Discarded her as if she were trash. As if her life meant nothing. Her fingers clawed at the frozen ground and snow, pulling herself out slowly, crawling towards the pavement. Coming back was harder than dying. Gwen had to get used to the weight of her limbs again, get used to the feel of the night air nipping at her skin.

She wasn't exactly human, so these trivial things didn't slow her down for long. Once she got to her feet, she could feel Hecate's magic guiding her towards her targets. She hadn't come back to this world as a victim or as a survivor. Now she was a blade. An instrument of something older and darker than the wickedness in the hearts of men. And she was strong and unafraid.

The hounds waited for her in the middle of the road, their coats melting into the shadows and their eyes reflecting like moonstone. Gwen scratched them behind their ears and they pressed their wet noses against her palm. "What do you think boys? Is it time to go home?"

The hounds howled and the sound carried like a whistling wind. She smiled as she melted into the shadows with them.

"Yeah. I thought so too."

Jesse hadn't left the cabin. Was it out of fear or remorse? Gwen touched the edge of the window and frost spread over the panes. She left her hand there until the whole cabin was covered in ice. It resembled a gingerbread house covered in icing with its doors and windows frozen shut. Something dies at the end of a relationship, too.

Tonight that would be Jesse.

Gwen went through the walls of the cabin and into the bedroom where Jesse lay sleeping. He was curled on his side, oblivious to her standing over him, watching him. *How could he sleep so peacefully after what we went through? How could he rest knowing what was done to me?*

The old Gwen would've been upset. She would've cried. Maybe blamed herself. But looking at him now, Gwen felt nothing but fury.

She crouched down so she was face to face with him. "Jesse. Wake up, Jesse."

When he stirred but didn't wake, Gwen slapped him across the face. Her voice reverberated through the room loud enough to make his ears bleed. "I said wake up!"

Jesse shot out of bed like his ass was on fire. The bedsheets twisted around his legs like vines and he tripped, landing on his back. He stared up at her, his grey eyes bulging out and his mouth gaping like a fish. She stalked towards him and he screamed.

"Be careful, Lover, or you'll let the Devil in. But I guess you already did, didn't you?"

Jesse shut his eyes. "Gwen. You're not real. This is just a nightmare. Go away."

The words sounded practiced. Like a mantra.

"Go away? Go away. That's all you ever wanted me to do, isn't it? You didn't want a girlfriend. You wanted a maid or a whore or a slave, but you never wanted me. You never appreciated *me*. Clean this, Gwen. Cook this, Gwen. Pay this, Gwen. Suck this, Gwen. You made me so fucking pathetic. So you're right, I am a goddamn nightmare. I'll be the worst nightmare you've ever had, baby, right up until the moment you die."

Jesse untangled himself and ran for it. As her fury grew, so did her form. Shadows climbed the walls, spread up over the ceiling, her words becoming louder and her voice getting deeper until he couldn't see where he was going. He bashed his shins into the coffee table and one the hounds snarled in his face. Jesse leapt backwards.

"What the fuck?"

Gwen spoke up from her seat on the couch. "I got some new pets. I think that's okay, seeing as you're the one who got Dax killed. Did they even bury him? Or did you?"

"I buried him, okay? I couldn't leave him out there like that."

Gwen glared. "Oh, but you were okay with what they did to me. Do you even know? Did you even ask?"

"Of course I didn't ask."

"Did you care?"

"Of course I cared, Gwen. I loved you."

She scoffed. "Did you call the police after they left?"

Jesse looked away. "I couldn't do that. Scopas will kill me if I get the police involved."

Gwen's fury reignited. "I knew you wouldn't. You don't have to worry about him because I'm going to be the one to kill you."

Jesse shook his head, pacing on the other side of the coffee table. "I've gotta wake up."

Gwen appeared in front of him and shoved him done on the floor. The very spot where she'd died. "You are awake."

"That's not possible. You died. I watched you die."

The hounds were circling him now. They growled when he tried to move.

"You chose me to die."

She let the light back into the room. She wanted him to see her decaying body. She watched as he gazed at her in horror.

His teeth chattered when he spoke. The room must have been freezing by now. "I'm sorry. I didn't want to die like that. You would've made the same choice, Gwen."

"But the difference is, I would've called the police. I would've cared, and I wouldn't have thought about myself, Jesse. I would've thought about the people who'd miss you. All the things you didn't bother to do for me."

It was time. But why was this so hard? Gwen heard Hecate's voice.

Love is always the last to die.

Jesse could tell he wasn't going to like whatever she was thinking. "Gwen, I'm sorry."

"That isn't good enough anymore."

Jesse bolted for the door. He hammered on it as he tried and failed to get it open.

How would she do it? She thought about ripping out his heart, but she didn't like it. She had no interest in his heart anymore. Gwen crept up behind him, reached around, and took hold of his head.

"No. Please."

Snap.

A VERY ZOMBIE CHRISTMAS

RYAN COLLEY

"'*T*was the night before Christmas, when all through the house, not a creature was stirring, not even a mouse," Tom whispered gently to his wide-eyed daughter in a sing-song voice. "The stockings were hung by the chimney with care, in hopes that St. Nicholas soon would be–"

"Tom, stop. We spoke about this, you'll scare her," Lucy reprimanded , her brow furrowed in annoyance. "This isn't the world for that anymore."

"Oh, come on," Tom laughed. "There's always time for Christmas. Besides, she's too small to even understand what I'm saying. It's just a rhyme for her."

"Tom. I do *not* want to hear it," Lucy said, raising her voice. She didn't shout, but the slightly-louder-than-a-whisper was enough for Tom to know she was angry. She'd never risk their safety by truly shouting, but those few octaves difference spoke volumes.

"Ok, fine. We won't celebrate Christmas," Tom relented, shoulders sagging. He added hopefully, "But we can reconsider next year?"

Lucy gripped the edge of the chair she stood beside, knuckles white, before also relenting and nodded. "Next year."

Tom smiled, walked across the candlelit room and embraced his wife, who tenderly wrapped her arms around him in return.

"I know you're scared. You have every right to be. The world is awful, or it was. But we haven't seen any of the undead for months. Not once. No signs of the living either," Tom whispered gently, holding her close. "What happened to Sally and Laura was horrible."

"Please don't say their names," Lucy interrupted, tears welling in her eyes before spilling out and down her cheeks.

Tom squeezed her and continued, "I'll never forget what happened, and I know you won't either. But we shouldn't feel guilty for being happy. We've survived. We're still surviving. And they'd want us to do more than survive. They'd want us to live. After everything we've seen, don't you think we deserve to be happy? Don't you think Clarissa deserves to be happy?"

Lucy looked to their daughter, who babbled quietly to herself in her rocker, content in the world and unaware of the horrors in the preceding years. She'd never know the panic in the early days as the cities fell to the dead, or the Government firebombing London, or how people killed each other without question to survive. Their daughter was a shining beacon of hope for the future of their new world. So pure and untainted, free from seeing the world she knew destroyed – she'd live to build a better world. She did deserve to be happy, one of them had to be, because Lucy knew Tom and herself would never truly be happy again. How could they, after everything they'd seen?

"Next year, I promise," Lucy said quietly, both for Tom and herself. The following year would be when they celebrated. Just one more year, then they could be happy.

Tom and Lucy put Clarissa to sleep in their bedroom – it was safer to sleep together in case someone or something got in. Besides, it was the only room they soundproofed when they were looking for somewhere for Lucy to give birth. Rugs, insulation foam, blankets and heavy curtains covering every surface did the job brilliantly. It shielded them from bringing the outside world crashing in, drawn by her screams of pain and exertions during labour.

The second-floor apartment they called home was never intended to be their home either. Simply a defendable location where Lucy could give birth. It was above a shop for one, which meant there were supplies they could take when needed. Every door and window on the ground floor had shutters or bars to protect the shop from pre-apocalypse break-ins, which worked in their post-apocalypse favour. They planned to move on after the birth and keep heading north where it was meant to be safer, but they enjoyed the safety they'd found. It was cosy, and they made it homely. Lucy recovered from the birthing peacefully, and Tom would collect supplies from the shop below or from the surrounding area when they needed it. It wasn't long following the birth of Clarissa – well, immediately after – that they realised how much a baby could cry, and the soundproofed room then had a new purpose.

Time dragged on and both of them knew they should move on, yet neither of them brought it up, both counting their blessings they had another day safely behind concrete walls. And, despite having a newborn to look after, they were able to sleep peacefully at night for the first time since the dead started walking. Not just because of the mental and physical security the walls and bars offered, but because of the quiet of their soundproofed bedroom. They hadn't realised how disruptive the ambient sounds of the apocalypse were to their sleep – distant gunshots and the eternal moaning of the undead made for a horrific soundtrack to life. It was something they'd gotten used to on a conscious level, but the psychological torment they suffered as a result was profound.

So with physical, mental and psychological peace of mind now available to them, they decided to make it their home. Not temporarily, or for the time being, but forever. After all, why would they leave real safety to find an imagined safety they'd only heard rumours about? They made adjustments to their accommodation to make it a better living space and took out any undead who wandered too close. And, before long, they were at the Christmas Eve that sparked their debate. Only a small thing in the grand scheme of life, but something that mattered a great deal to Tom. He wanted their daughter to have happy memories, and he knew Lucy did as well. He just had to show her how much it mattered. He knew that she wouldn't change her mind by the following Christmas, but he knew seeing the joy that Christmas brought their daughter would be enough to change it. He just had to show her.

When Clarissa and Lucy were finally asleep, Tom got out of bed as silently as possible. Not that the volume of his movement mattered when he and Lucy had both spent so long fearing for their lives day and night. Any noise in close proximity was enough to trigger them.

"Where y'going?" Lucy murmured, halfway between the land of the consciousness and the realm of twilight, yet still reaching for the weapon she kept by her bedside.

"Just going to the loo," Tom answered as he bent down and kissed Lucy on the forehead, before doing the same to Clarissa. As he was leaving the room, he took a last-second glance at the two most beautiful people in his life, before closing the door behind him.

Tom made his way to the toilet – he wasn't lying after all. He really did need to go, but it wasn't his end destination. He squatted on the toilet, emptying himself in preparation for what was to come. He didn't pull the flush – not because they were out of water, they'd been filling the cistern with river water and dealing with their waste that way – but because he didn't want to wake Lucy again. He'd flush when he was back and, in Lucy's sleep-addled brain, she wouldn't know how long he'd been away.

Once he was done in the toilet, he dug his clothes back out of the wash basket, specifically picking darker clothes, and slipped them back on. He ignored the whiff of milky baby vomit that hit him and put on his climbing shoes – something he found in a sports store for rock climbing. However, they were excellent for climbing walls and scaling the sides of buildings while looking for supplies. On top of that, they made moving silently easy, unlike his hiking boots that were good for long distances but reduced his foot dexterity. He couldn't afford to be stomping around at night. Sure, he was certain there weren't any zombies in the area any longer, but advantages didn't hurt. The darker clothes were a perfect example of that. They made great camouflage in the dark of the night, even more so since there weren't any street lamps active and the moon was obscured by cloud cover.

His final addition was his utility belt that Lucy frequently laughed at whenever he wore it, but it didn't stop him feeling like Batman every time he put it on. it wasn't bright yellow like the pointy-eared hero he still secretly worshipped, but it had a lot of pouches filled with various potentially life-saving items. Firecrackers and a lighter in one pouch, a perfect distraction in the right circumstance. A paracord in another, which could be used in a variety of ways, including tying door handles together to create a temporary safe room from the pursuing undead. A standard multitool was nestled in another pouch – twenty different tools for hundreds of uses! An axe hung from a loop, a standard means to protect oneself in the end times. A flashlight hung from another loop for good measure – there were a lot of dark buildings with the electricity off. Another had a small bottle of cleaning solution for wounds, made of bleach and water. It wasn't exactly pharmaceutically safe, but it did the job. And the final pouch? A lock of his daughter's hair – a constant reminder of his need to keep fighting.

With all the gear he needed about his person, he poured a small thimble of condensed milk into a glass – they couldn't spare a lot – and then took a bite out of a stale cookie he'd been saving for such an occasion. He placed both on the dining table in a very theatrical fashion along with a note he'd written earlier in the week. He nodded to himself with a smile – a job well done – before moving on.

With the final touch complete, he knew it was time to set out. He opened the window at the front of their home that exited onto the overhang of the store below. It was his standard way in and out of the building – they hadn't unlocked the front door for months. It helped him train his muscles so that he could move more vertically when he was out looking for supplies. Plus it ensured that the ground floor was always locked up and they lived in the safety that the undead couldn't climb.

Tom made his way to the edge of the overhang, quickly checking the immediate for any undead that he knew wouldn't be there, and gripped the nearby lamppost before climbing down it with a well-practised precision and ease. He'd return the same way when he was back as well, climbing back up and into the safety of his home.

Once his feet met the concrete of the pavement below, Tom made one last cursory glance around before moving onwards. He wasn't out searching for supplies or on a scouting mission; he had a specific goal in mind.

Tom had explored the area of the town they called home many times before while scavenging supplies – mainly sticking to places where essentials would likely be, such as supermarkets and pharmacies. In recent times, as things in stores dwindled, he'd started exploring houses and homes. It wasn't as lucrative, but they were definitely moving into more desperate times. All that being said, what he was looking for wasn't in a supermarket or home, but he knew it was exactly where it was.

He'd spotted the particular location he was looking for that Christmas Eve in the early days of his exploration. He didn't know what he would find on his return, simply because he hadn't needed to pass that way in a while. However, he couldn't see any reason it would be looted. It wasn't essential to survival and that's all people worried about anymore.

Tom moved quietly through the town – not as quietly as he had done when they first moved to the area, but there were a lot of zombies in those days. On his stroll through the crisp night air, he didn't see any undead. Nor any signs of the living. A small, smug smile spread over his lips as he basked in his own correctness. He watched the town from his window almost every day and never saw movement. Lucy was worried about nothing. His casual and uninterrupted jaunt proved that.

Before long, Tom found what he was looking for, a small store on the outskirts of town. A toy store – Lucky's Toy Emporium. Where all toys were handcrafted and dreams come true, or that's what the sign said, anyway. The glass front was untouched, and why wouldn't it be? No one was looting toys in the apocalypse. Well, no one except for Tom .

Tom pushed his face against the glass, trying to peer into the darkness within to see if he could make out anything. He couldn't see much besides the fact the store still looked untouched. He tried the door, which opened without resistance. It must have been unlocked since the pre-apocalypse. With one last look around him, he grinned and walked inside, a small bell announcing his arrival.

Tom let the door close quietly behind him, softening its closure with his hand. Once it was shut, he stood unmoving in the darkness and breathed the stale air while he listened. There was a faint undertone of rot, but that was common in the apocalypse. He didn't hear any movement, nor any moaning of the undead. That was lucky for him. When he was sure enough time had passed for any attackers to reveal themselves, he pulled out the flashlight from his utility belt and flicked it to life, illuminating the shelves in a bluish light.

Still without moving forward, he moved the beam of his light around the store and checked out his surroundings. It was a small store, not very wide, with only one set of shelves running down the middle to form two short aisles. The shelves were crammed with unique and beautiful wooden toys. Each painted or carved differently to the one beside it. There were small cars and rockets, full-sized tricycles and bikes, dollhouses both big and small. All would be quite cumbersome to carry back, and wooden toys could be noisy if thrown by a boisterous toddler. So Tom wanted something smaller and softer. Something their daughter would be able to keep with her for years.

So Tom began moving amongst the toys, looking at each one with a smile – almost forgetting he was in the end times. He moved deeper into the store, admiring everything as he went, until he saw exactly what he was looking for. Behind the counter, on a shelf by itself, was a palm-sized, hand-stitched doll. She had long red hair made from strands of wool, button eyes, and tiny, sewed on overalls. It was perfect! Tom silently fist pumped the air for a successful find and leaned across the counter to swipe it off the shelf. No sooner had his hand crossed the void behind the counter did another hand appear from the darkness below and grab his wrist.

Tom let out a yelp of surprise and then a cry of pain as an elderly undead man sa nk his broken, rotten teeth into him. Momentary panic took over Tom as he tried to shake the zombie loose. Instead of freeing himself, his shaking caused more flesh to tear away from his wrist, causing the man to finally relent and hungrily devour what small piece he'd managed to get.

Jumping back from the attacker, Tom examined his wrist as he took out the cleaning solution with the other hand. It wasn't deep, even if it was bleeding a lot, but he learned long ago that bites weren't harmful if cleaned quickly. People died and came back regardless of a bite – he just had to stop an infection setting in. Tom had a few brief moments to act, not because of the bite, but because the elder zombie was now on his feet and heading towards him.

Tom pulled off the lid to the solution and poured it over his wound. The bleach-water mixture caused pain to shoot along his nervous system, but at least it did its job. Archaic yet efficient. He cast the container to one side and withdrew his axe.

"Lucky, I presume?" Tom asked the zombie sarcastically, grabbing the undead man by his extended hand and yanking the zombie towards him. The zombie stumbled forward and past Tom, colliding with the shelving down the middle of the store. Toys and shelves collapsed with an ear-shattering noise as the zombie was sprawled in the debris of his life's work. It was a simple technique, especially since the undead had poor coordination, and meant he would be able to take him out from a safer angle.

Tom moved in, not waiting a second longer than he had t o, and struck him with the axe twice. The first cleaved through the rotting, grey face of the once-man, turning his inhuman snarl into something far more ghastly as his face ripped in two. He ignored the dark ichor leaking from the man and the foetid smell that filled the air as it escaped him. The second strike splintered the skull and destroyed what-ever was left of the grey matter within, finally ending the unlife.

Wiping his axe off on the dead man, Tom stopped to catch his breath as the dust settled from the collapsing shelves. He'd been caught off guard – there was no simple way about. He'd become relaxed in his safety and too arrogant. He mentally berated himself for getting lazy and then laughed – Lucy was going to give him hell. Smiling to himself, Tom fetched the doll and stuck it in his pocket before heading for the door.

Opening the door, Tom caught movement out of the corner of his eye from the alley opposite. He froze, eyes darting towards the source of what he saw. It was a zombie. Tom knew it would be alright, it was only one. If he couldn't kill it, he could easily outrun it. He was more surprised to see a second zombie after so long.

Moving to head outside, Tom saw movement again, this time from the direction he was meant to be heading. More zombies – a lot more – were disgorging themselves from open doorways. He shook his head in disbelief. Where had they all come from? Had they been hiding? Hibernating? Why were they coming out now? He looked behind him at the collapsed shelves. Had the noise of his conflict pushed them back into action? Had it finally given them enough stimulation to move again?

He looked in the direction of the alley from where the lone zombie had exited, liking his odds of taking out one zombie and taking a detour to get home as opposed to the twenty or so zombies on the direct route. Except, it wasn't a single zombie anymore. That one zombie was the head of a macabre black parade of the undead as more and more filtered out from behind.

"Shit," Tom hissed, fear gripping his chest as he fought off the need to hyperventilate. He was surrounded. He lit up his firecrackers and threw them as far as he could. They soared through the air, crackling and letting off light as they landed.

And it worked, but only for a few moments. They had their eyes on fresh food and some overcompensating sparklers weren't going to change that.

Fighting to keep the panic at bay, he headed back inside the store to look for something. Anything. There was no back-door out of the store, no side window, no air vent or basement he could retreat to. Instead, Tom used the paracord to tie the door shut, but he knew that wouldn't stop them. All Tom could do was watch his slowly approaching death through the glass front of the door. He readied his axe and clutched his daughter's lock of hair. A quiet beep from his watch let him know it was midnight.

"Merry Christmas, Clarissa," Tom whispered, tears rolling down his face, as the glass shattered and the oncoming wave of undead poured into the store and swallowed him.

Lucy didn't know what the time was, but she awoke to the soft sounds of Clarissa babbling to herself and the realisation that Tom wasn't in bed beside her. That wasn't unusual – he sometimes got up early to make breakfast or exercise. Lucy smiled, it was Christmas after all. She climbed out of bed and scooped up Clarissa.

"Can you say da-da?" Lucy asked her daughter in the same voice that came instinctually to all parents when talking to their children. "Da-da?"

Clarissa giggled and continued babbling. Lucy kept talking to her, asking her questions that she had no possible way to comprehend – yet they communicated, mother and daughter.

Carrying their child, Lucy wandered out into their main living area. Still no sign of Tom. Lucy called his name as loudly as she dared, but there was no answer. Lucy placed Clarissa in her rocker and began to explore the rest of their apartment. It wasn't a big space, so it wasn't like Tom could be hiding.

Lucy noticed the half-eaten cookie and milk on the table. She smiled momentarily, rolling her eyes at Tom, before spotting the note. Picking it up, Lucy began to read it aloud – it was definitely Tom's writing, yet had more of a flourish to it.

"Dear Clarissa, I hope my letter finds you well! I hear you've been a very good girl this year and I know your mummy and daddy are very proud of you. So I've worked very hard to get you this present. Thank you for the milk and cookie. From Father Christmas."

Lucy finished reading the letter, her playful smile slowly disappearing as her face drained of colour and warmth as she read those final words. A present? What present? No, Tom wouldn't have gone out to get a present. That was crazy.

Lucy dropped the letter and started racing through the apartment, checking every room and emptying everything she found, looking for something that would reveal the truth. Anything that told her one way or the other. And she found it – or didn't find it as the case was. His utility belt was gone – he never left without it. And she realised that was the truth. She knew he'd gone out into the world to try and make their daughter happy.

Lucy collapsed into the chair. Tears filled her eyes and

spilled out and down her cheeks. She couldn't handle the world by herself. She needed Tom – Clarissa did too. How would they carry on without him? She fell into a long silence, which was only broken as Clarissa finally said her first words.

"Da-da?"

5

CHRISTMAS HARVEST

LILY LUCHESI

"Ugh!" Jessica Klaus slapped her desk with her hand, making her laptop shake. "Another one! I swear, I am so damn sick of this."

"Article on us again?" her husband, Nick, guessed.

"What else?" She sighed, clicking the red X in the top right corner. Her wallpaper, which was a panorama of their home all covered in snow, popped up. A fire burned in the grate, which you could see through the window.

"What was it about this time?" he asked, handing her a cup of blood with peppermint liqueur added in. Very Christmas-y.

"It was the attached depiction of you. For the love of everything, these people have never seen you, so how do they all picture you the same way? What asshat said, 'hey, I bet this guy is eighty, fat, and laughs like a loon'? Whomever it was, I'd like to set a scorpion on their dick."

Nick laughed, choking on his drink a little. "Damn, you're

really pissed this year. Sweetheart, calm down, before we have a repeat of nineteen-fifty-three."

Jessica smirked, her blood-red lips parting to reveal her sharp fangs. She could retract them, but preferred to leave them.

1953 was a time of year when parents were allowed to beat their children, and husbands were allowed to beat their wives without reprimand. In fact, it was actually socially acceptable to do both! In 1953, people who were gay were being chemically castrated. Women were property and had no jobs; if they did, they were treated with contempt that they were not taking care of their families. It was a pretty shitty year, and Jessica had enough, "punishing" the cruel people. She fed quite well that night, fueling the ridiculous story of "Krampus". It had been their most bountiful Harvest to date.

However, the complications that arose from so many deaths had nearly been catastrophic. The loved ones of the deceased noticed a pattern, and it had been terrifying for Nick, to think that his beautiful wife was going to be hunted and their true secret was going to be out.

"Fifty-three was a lovely year." She stood up, stretching. Her long, white hair hung to her waist, brushed back from her heart-shaped face. "I assume this is the last from last year's Harvest?" She gestured to her mug.

Nick nodded, his spiky white hair not moving. "Glad we can get more tomorrow."

Jessica sat next to him, their black and red clothes matching perfectly, as they always did. "You want me to come and help?"

Nick smiled wryly. "You have a tendency to get a bit overzealous during the yearly Harvest."

She pouted, but couldn't hold the expression for long. She draped herself in Nick's lap, and he stroked her pale skin, which really stood out under her black clothes and cosmetics. She was so beautiful, it made him ache to look at her. She was also the brains of their operation, which was why he couldn't stay mad at her for long. She was the reason that they two had survived when the rest of their species had been wiped out, by creating a mythical persona for them both, effectively cloaking them from humans in fantasy.

"Have you forgotten that it was my idea to trade toys for our nourishment?" she asked. "After all, these silly little mortals give up their time, their money, and sometimes their lives for material items. I figured it was an even trade. And I was right ... as usual."

He sighed. "Yes, you were right. Speaking of, the imps have given us our stock for tomorrow night. Already inventoried and everything. They just need to bring it outside on the carriage."

"Have you seen their depiction of the imps?" Jessica asked, back on her earlier complaint. He was used to this: it happened the same time every year.

"Yes, I have. I am actually delivering a few copies of *The Elf on the Shelf*." Nick laughed. "Oh, what would happen if they saw the imps?"

"Years of nightmares and therapy ... how delicious their fear would be!" Jessica laughed. "Please let me come with you. They won't be expecting a woman, and how I so love to taste their fear!"

Nick finally relented. "Yeah, sure. Just don't go overboard, okay?"

She pretended to cross her heart as she put her black trench coat on. "I'll go check the wolves!"

Nick could see her through the window, checking all twelve of their precious pets. She bent down, giving them treats, and petting their scruff. As gentle as if they were a gaggle of golden retrievers ... or reindeer. He peered harder, seeing that they were eating bits of greyish imp flesh. He smirked. Looked like Jessica finally got around to punishing the imp who had screwed up when painting that one doll's face.

This was a business, and in business you couldn't afford such errors.

He checked the clock. The sun was setting in Australia. His schedule was always perfect, and he would start in Australia, slowly heading westward till he finished with America. Always beating the sun; always carrying home a heavier sleigh than when he started out, even after all the toys had been deposited: payment for a service the children did not know they rendered. With Jessica coming with him, he was certain that this year's sleigh would be even heavier on the return trip. She could promise to behave all she wanted, but he knew he could not restrain her when the Harvest was happening. If it didn't risk their discovery, he wouldn't want to restrain her.

"Darlin', make sure they're fed quickly: it's almost time to go," he called, head out the front door as the icy cold wind nipped at his nose.

"Already done," Jessica called, walking back towards him.

Her pale cheeks were reddened by the wind and he thought about the mortal depiction of them both, with their feverish faces. He guessed that was at least partially correct. "The imps are still finishing the packing. If they were any slower, they'd be going backwards!"

Nick donned his hat and cloak to triple guard against the frigid night sky as he readied the wolves. His and Jessica's innate abilities were enough to make the carriage fly, but they needed extra muscle to make it move, which was where their beloved wolves came in. Aside, Nick loved the sound of their howls in the wind.

Before completely exiting the house and locking up, he went into the den and took out their beloved pet, Rudy. He was a Mexican Free-Tailed Bat, the fastest flyer of the species, and they kept him healthy and warm in their home, only letting him into the freezing temperatures one night a year.

Jessica came up and gently took Rudy from him. Despite her homicidal urges, she was the sweetest, most loving person towards animals. He never loved her more than when he saw her taking care of their pets.

She cooed to Rudy as she walked outside to attach him to his custom made harness. There was no better navigator in the darkest hours of the night than a bat with echolocation. Rudy might not look like the humans' depiction of him, but Nick thought he was pretty adorable.

He went to the workshop and saw that the imps were indeed nearly ready, but they were certainly cutting it close with their poor time management. They were constantly whining, arguing with him about their jobs.

Nick kept them with all the meat they could eat after the

Harvest had been brought back, made sure their lodging was as hot as where they came from, and never really badgered them to do more work than necessary, even though their contracts said that he could if he wanted to. Lucifer was a hard taskmaster compared with the job Nick gave them.

Grey-skinned creatures, anywhere between two and three feet tall with three-toed clawed feet, four sharp-tipped clawed fingers, nought but skin and bones, with bulging black eyes like a fly's, they were not the most appealing creatures to behold. Some of them had one eye, some had as many as six. Their noses were either flat like a pig's or long like a tree branch and their wide, no-lipped mouths were filled with piranha-sharp teeth. They had large, bat-like ears. They were genderless, wore no clothes, and spent their free time torturing polar bears for fun, dining on them afterwards.

"Come on, time's running short," Nick said, ushering a few of them out with the massive overstuffed bags of toys. He followed the last one back to the carriage. Jessica had last updated it in the mid nineteenth century with a carriage from London. Black-canopied and made of black iron, it had once been used as a hearse before mechanical vehicles were invented. It was fitting for their objective, that it had once transported dead mortal bodies.

In the back was a large space with more than enough room for their trip, both outgoing and returning, and their bounty. Harvesting required patience, stealth, and a lot of storage space for the journey around the Western world. Black silk curtains with black lace covered the carriage so none could see inside if they happened to be spotted.

She was waiting for him, already sitting shotgun with

their schedule and list of names in hand. He swore, if not for Jessica, he'd never get anything done. She was brilliant.

"Ready, love?" she asked as he approached, petting each wolf in turn and calling them by their names. "Careful, Donner's got a bite to him today. We might have to feed one of the parents to him to keep him content tonight."

Nick settled himself in his seat and took the reins in his black-gloved hands. He whipped them to get the wolves going as Jessica assisted with her magic. Within a few moments they were flying away from the South Pole, heading south to Australia, where after they would keep heading west until they returned home, the Harvest completed for the next three-hundred and sixty-four days.

For quite some time, all through Australia, most of Europe, and the United Kingdom, Jessica was calm and restrained herself as she left the presents for the children while Nick went upstairs to take their payment from the tiny, sleeping bodies.

It wasn't until they reached halfway across the United States that Jessica began to get fidgety, as he knew she would. She controlled her hunger admirably, but even Nick knew that neither of them could get through this night without sampling their Harvest while fresh.

They were in a large house in a midwestern suburb when she finally lost control. She flung the wrapped gifts down carelessly, also knocking over the plate of now soured milk and crumbly sugar cookies that had been left out for her husband. That was certainly not the snack either of them came here for. She followed Nick upstairs, where the family's four children were all asleep.

"Four! I could never imagine having one ... for more than dinner, anyway," Jessica said, her red eyes glowing in the darkness of the bedroom. She giggled, looking down at the children. Twin girls were sleeping soundlessly in their frilly pink beds, clad in equally frilly white nightgowns. "It's amazing how children sleep like the truly dead when they've engorged themselves on sweets." She ran her black-lacquered nail along the bedspread. "And they even left us a matching set."

Nick was about to say that they shouldn't do this, that it was wrong, it could expose them, and on and on. It would all be true, but oh, how he did miss dining on fresh blood as opposed to the preserved stock they were currently Harvesting. They could only do this one night a year, after all, and he was a mere immortal.

In the silence of the Witching Hour, he could hear the sound of their blood sluggishly moving through their veins, its vivacity dulled by the deep slumber unique to small children.

He watched Jessica as she bent down and picked up the little girl, who was barely three years old. The child fussed for a moment before falling back asleep in his wife's arms. Jessica smiled, her fangs on full display once again. She gestured silently for him to take the other girl. She mouthed, *Before the sun rises, Nick.*

And he watched as she bent her head down to the soft flesh at the throat of a child that had not even shed her baby fat, sinking her fangs into it. The smell of freshly spilled blood permeated the air, driving Nick nearly mad with bloodlust.

Fast as a snake descending on a mouse, he slunk forward and picked up the other little girl. She was startled by the sudden movement and when she laid eyes first on Nick and then on Jessica, with her mouth covered in blood and fangs buried in her twin's neck. The little girl began to cry.

Her screams didn't even reach a high enough volume to rouse her parents or siblings before Nick felt his fangs pierce her sleep-warmed flesh. Fear made her heart begin to beat faster, pumping the sweet, iron-tinged blood quickly down his throat, filling him in a way that no Harvested blood ever could.

Power thrummed in his veins and his cold, Undead body was warmed as he felt the child's heartbeat flicker. He tore his fangs from her flesh, tearing the skin like an animal, before he took her head in his hands and twisted, breaking her neck. He dropped the body back onto the bed, the girl's lifeless eyes staring at the ceiling, a glassy mimic of the doll's that he had left under the Christmas tree.

Jessica was smiling over at him, still holding the other girl by the pigtails in one hand. Her lips were dripping with fresh blood, drops speckling her cleavage. He imagined his face looked as ghoulish as hers did were a mortal to see him, but to him she was more than beautiful.

"Bring their bodies for the wolves?" Nick asked.

Jessica nodded, chuckling. She walked over to him, dragging the girl behind her like a ragdoll. She leaned up and kissed him, the blood on their lips mingling together, smearing on their faces.

"And to think," she whispered, her voice a deep, raspy purr, "they call you a saint."

They brought the girls' still warm bodies to the rooftop, where the wolves and Rudy were waiting with their carriage. Nick tossed one corpse to the six in the back of the line, and Jessica handed hers to the ones near the front, but only after cupping her hands in the bit of blood she'd left in the body, bringing them to Rudy to let him drink.

The frigid air no longer bothered them, warmed as they now were. The back of the carriage rocked, their youthful captives trying fruitlessly to escape. Nick could hear the gallons of blood sloshing with their movements. Their Harvest was half bottled, half freshly preserved, as it always was. The half moon shone down on them all, fresh snow littered the roof, only marred by the blood and gore from the wolves' feeding.

Jessica was smiling and humming as she licked her palm clean. "Merry Christmas, dear Saint Nicholas."

Nick winked. "Merry Christmas, my love."

6

GIFT OF CAROLS

AMIR LANE

Chapter 1

*T*here was something about Christmastime that simultaneously brought out the best and worst in people. Charity drives were rampant, but so were sirens using their second sets of vocal cords to influence people into giving a little more than they normally would, even in the 'season of giving'.

There was no reason for them to call a detective to handle the issue, especially not me. The Toronto Police department who would have been much better at handling this than me. I could hold my own against most parahumans, but even with the protective rings on my fingers and the barriers moving beneath my skin, I didn't like the idea of going head-to-head with them without any backup. The only reason I was out here was because the siren requested me by name, and told the responding officer that not only was she one of my informants from when I worked Homicide, but that she was working undercover for me at that very moment.

I made sure to refill my travel mug with fresh coffee before heading out the door. If nothing else, getting out of the precinct would help me clear my head before I went back to working on real cases.

"Dasia, *habibti,* you can't tell people you're working for me. And you *shouldn't* tell people you were one of my informants," I said, uncuffing her hands from behind her back.

Dasia might not have been a strictly law-abiding citizen, but she was fairly harmless as far as sirens went.

"Well, I'm working for the greater good! It's not worse than the lottery or casinos, you know. You aren't going to take me in, are you, Detective Arshad? Not over a silly thing like this. It's Christmas!"

There were still two weeks until Christmas, but that didn't matter. From the day after Halloween, it was Christmas in this country. I sighed, pinching the bridge of my nose. I wanted to let her go, but this wasn't the first time she'd done something like this. One of these days, she was going to get herself hurt.

"I can't let you go around breaking the law. Not even for a good cause, *or* for Christmas."

Dasia shifted from foot to foot. Her bare hands were balled into fists, though there was no sign of hostility in her posture.

I sighed again and pulled my purple leather gloves lined with sheep's wool off. Toronto had fairly mild winters compared to most of Canada, but it was still much colder than Lebanon, where I had grown up. The cold immediately began to chill the rings on my fingers. I offered the gloves out to Dasia. She blinked up at me and took them.

"Detective—"

The ringing of my phone interrupted whatever she was about to say. I held up a finger that was quickly going numb and pulled it from my pocket. Rowan Oak's name was stretched across the screen. He was a texter, so if he was calling, it had to be important.

"I have to take this." I swiped my thumb across the screen. "Arshad speaking."

"Hey, it's me. You busy right now?"

My eyes flickered to Dasia, rubbing her now-gloved hands together. Either purple suited her, or the smile on her face did.

"It's nothing that can't wait. What's going on?"

On the other end of the line, Rowan clicked a pen. "You know all those teenagers that've gone missing the past few weeks?"

"Of course."

Even if it hadn't been all over the news, it was all anybody in the precinct would talk about. Four teenage boys had gone missing from the Weston neighborhood this month. They'd all been taken from their homes with no signs of forced entry and no sign that they'd simply run away.

"One of them just turned up. Missing Persons and Homicide want your opinion on the body."

I scratched my nose with my short, acrylic nails. They were metallic red for the season. Dasia watched me and strained to hear the conversation with all the subtlety of a moose on a hockey rink.

"Let me guess. It's weird?" I asked rhetorically.

It had to be. The only body cases I handled these days were 'weird' ones. My days of dealing with corpses were supposed to be over. My boss disagreed.

"Oh, it always is. I'll meet you at the lab in twenty. Bring coffee."

With that, the line went dead. I tucked my phone back into my pocket and turned my attention back to Dasia's expectant expression. She now dropped low on my priority list.

"You're right," I said. I shouldn't have been encouraging her, but I pulled my wallet from the bottom of my jacket pocket. The only bills I had were green 20s. I handed one to her. "It's Christmas. This is your last warning. Let's not have this conversation again."

"Your gloves—!"

I waved my hand dismissively as I crossed the street.

"Keep them. Stay warm, Dasia."

I spent three years as a Homicide detective before transferring to Special Crimes a few months ago. That made me the 12th Precinct's leading expert in what Rowan called 'weird body shit'. It also meant that every time a strange body was found, I was the one who got called in to investigate.

It didn't bother me as much as I pretended it did. Though I didn't think I'd ever said so out loud, I'd never wanted to leave Homicide. I loved solving murders, and I was good at it. The only reason I transferred to Special Crimes was because it was what my girlfriend, Ariadne, blamed for most of the problems in our relationship. She wasn't entirely wrong. Knowing that any minute I wasn't working was a minute a murderer was using to get away aggravated my workaholic tendencies to the point that I worked 16-hour days and weekends. There hadn't been a day where I didn't take a case home. It wasn't healthy.

It was her or Homicide, and I chose her.

I didn't regret it for one minute. Special Crimes presented its own challenges, and there was no shortage of unusual bodies turning up in Toronto. Even in a relatively quiet neighborhood like Weston, there was at least one a month. Usually, Rowan helped with those cases. Our co-detectives always pulled rank to avoid dealing with them.

There wasn't much snow on the ground despite it being a week into December. Toronto winters were milder than the ones up north. Today was warm enough that I could roll down my window as I drove to the Forensic Services and Coroner's Complex. It was a short enough drive, but I had to take a bit of a detour to get Rowan's coffee.

Rowan was already waiting for me in the examination room. A man of many words, he nodded to me in greeting.

"Bless you," he said, taking the paper cup from me.

With one of my hands free, I pulled off my spare leather gloves — black, not purple — and tucked them into my pocket. They were finally starting to warm up from being in the car all day.

"Where is the examiner?" I asked.

"On her way. Don't be disappointed, Deva says this isn't the weirdest body we've handled."

I rolled my eyes. As if I would be disappointed by that. With Christmas approaching, I had more than enough to keep me busy without an impossible crime to solve. My family was Muslim, but we still celebrated Christmas, even if it was socially rather than religiously. My brothers were coming in from Boston and Thunder Bay with their families to celebrate, which meant I had to go to my parents' place in Ottawa a few days early to help make sure everything was ready. And since Ariadne wasn't able to take time off until Christmas Eve, I had to avoid questions on when we were getting married and starting a family of our own by myself.

I wasn't a person who gambled, but I was willing to bet my Evil Eye pendant that she was using work as an excuse to avoid the conversation herself. It was a good idea, and I didn't blame her.

Doctor Deva Jhaveri walked into the room with long, purposeful strides despite her short stature. A man I didn't recognize followed quickly at her heels.

"Detectives Oak and Arshad, Doctor Darlington. Doctor Darlington, Detectives Oak and Arshad," she said.

"Nice to meet you," I said, while Rowan only nodded and sipped his coffee.

Darlington returned the nod and smiled, revealing a set of sharp teeth in front of human ones.

"The victim is Neil Greyson. Seventeen years old. Cause of death is infection that caused necrosis to much of his body," Deva said.

She wasn't a woman who wasted time. It was one of the

things that made her my favourite medical examiner to work with.

"That's not so weird," Rowan said slowly.

"The cause of death is not strange. The cause of infection is."

Deva pulled back the sheet covering the body on the steel operating table to expose the upper half of the victim's body. My eyebrows rose, and Rowan whistled through his teeth.

"All right," he said, "I'll admit. *That* is weird."

A box of latex gloves sat on the wheeled table next to me. I removed the rings from my fingers, silently lamenting the feeling of the protective charms leaving my skin, and pulled on a pair of the blue gloves. My nails were getting long enough that I was worried about ripping them. I'd have to get them redone soon. I picked up a surgical mask from the same table and fixed the straps behind my ears.

Darlington stepped back to give me room to examine the body.

Some of the bones were broken, and both shoulders were dislocated. Chunks were missing from the corpse. My first thought was that they had been cut out but, when I leaned closer, I could make out the outline of teeth along the muscles and the bits of bone that were visible. While his face and neck were mostly intact, the bulk of his left arm had been eaten, and the right one was missing from below the elbow. Deep gashes lined his chest. The few chunks taken out of his abdomen suggested whatever had eaten him had either been interrupted or decided not to eat the rest of it.

"His legs?" I asked.

"Cleaned like chicken legs," Deva said.

"Oh, yeah, we should *totally* get a Homicide detective in Special Crimes," Rowan muttered sarcastically behind me. "Because you know what we don't get to see enough of? This shit."

"Detective Oak, there is a trash can behind you if you are going to be sick," Deva said.

Rowan huffed and folded his arms over his chest, but I didn't miss the way he inched toward the trash can. It was mostly his fault I was here. He was the one who'd recommended me for the transfer to this department.

"Do you know what made these bites?" I asked.

Darlington shook his head. "It doesn't match anything we've seen. We wanted you to see it first, but we'll get dental impressions from the bones. If we find a match to anything, you'll be the first to know."

The bite marks were strange enough. I had no idea what they were from, either. The shape of what little I could see didn't match a human jaw, and the teeth were obviously sharp. It wasn't the bites themselves that bothered me, but the rotten flesh surrounding them.

"That's gross," Rowan said as he peered over the body, evidently deciding he wasn't going to be sick.

"That's not the worst part of it," Darlington said.

I raised an eyebrow. *This* wasn't the worst part of it?

"What's the worst part?" I asked, worried even as I spoke the words about what he was going to say.

What could *possibly* be worse?

Darlington gave a slight swallow and looked at Deva, either silently asking for permission to tell us or for her to tell us herself. He looked young enough that I wondered if this might have been one of his first autopsies. Of course, looking young didn't mean he *was* young. It was his attitude more than anything that gave the impression. Deva tipped her head slightly, and Darlington sighed.

"He was alive when these bites were taken."

My other eyebrow came up to meet the first. Rowan turned away with his hand over his mouth and a sound that suggested he was going to have to use that trash can after all.

Darlington was right. That was definitely worse.

Chapter 2

A pair of detectives waited for us in the hall when we stepped out of the examination room.

"Charleston Willoughby," the taller one said, stepping forward to shake Rowan's hand first, then mine. The bark coating his palm was coarse against my skin. "Missing Persons."

"Rowan Oak, Fairuz Arshad. I'm guessing you're Homicide?" Rowan said, nodding toward the second man.

The second man narrowed his eyes up at me from behind thick-rimmed glasses. I would have liked to say that his dislike for me was based solely on the fact that I towered over him. It wasn't my fault satyrs were short. Even with his horns, he only came to my shoulder, even when I was wearing flats. Truthfully, the dislike was professional as well. I didn't take it personally. If he didn't like me solving his cases while he spun around in circles hounding what was clearly the wrong perpetrator, that was his problem. Actually, since I'd transferred in March, it wasn't even his problem anymore.

I gave him a polite smile, which only served to deepen his scowl. As long as I didn't have to work with him, I didn't care if he didn't like me. If it affected this case, then I *would* be his problem.

"Detective Caledon, it's good to see you again," I said politely.

"I specifically told Staff Sergeant Beaupré I *didn't* want you working this case."

Rowan whistled through his teeth. "What'd you do, Arshad, steal his girlfriend?"

Caledon turned his glare to Rowan, who seemed unfazed as ever. Very little ever seemed to bother him. Five years as a Sex Crimes detective would do that. Sometimes, I could believe he'd seen worse things than I had. Certainly he'd seen worse than Caledon, who didn't leave his desk if he didn't have to.

If Rowan wasn't going to let Caledon get to him, neither would I.

Willoughby cleared his throat and gave Caledon a sideways pleading glance that deepened the lines around his eyes.

"Can we please keep this civil? We have one dead boy so far. It could be more. I'd like to find the culprit before another boy turns up."

"He's right," I said. "I'm sure we can work together on this."

"Special Crimes my special ass," Caledon muttered.

I left Homicide because of the effect it had on my health,

but detectives like Caledon hadn't exactly given me a compelling reason to stay. Dealing with him right now made me glad there were only five of us in my precinct's division, and that we all got along.

"The family is next door to talk to you," Willoughby said, tactfully ignoring Caledon.

By 'next door', Willoughby meant down the street. The 12th Precinct was only a few minutes' drive from the Coroner's Complex.

When we arrived, the parents were still in tears. Rowan pat my shoulder.

"Have fun in there, Homicide and Former Homicide. We'll watch from out here. Willoughby, you ever have Detective-Sergeant Harper's coffee? Oh, man, you are in for a *treat*."

I was pretty good at talking to victims and their families. I was sympathetic enough that they rarely felt defensive around me. The fact that I was human, even if I was a witch, might have helped.

This was the part I hated most about working in Homicide. Talking to the families never got easier. Caledon didn't help. He interrupted every time I spoke, glowered at me from behind his glasses, and huffed every time the mother took another tissue to blow her nose into. If I weren't trying to show a unified front with the cow, I would have kicked him.

Neil Greyson's parents called him a problem child. A good boy at heart, his mother insisted, but he'd gotten into some trouble lately. Before he disappeared, he'd left the house after fighting with his parents over stealing money from them to buy drugs. They'd been convinced he was going to return home any day. Even though he was lying on a slab fifteen minutes away, I didn't doubt they were still hoping.

"Problem child is an understatement," Rowan said when I decided we were done talking to them. He was flipping through a thin case file, Willoughby reading over his shoulder. "Been arrested three times, done a total of four months in juvie. Amazing, he tried to steal a cop car."

"I disagree with your definition of amazing," Caledon grunted.

I opened my mouth to tell him what I thought of *his* definition of amazing, but Rowan cut me off.

"I think we got enough to work with for now," he said quickly, pulling me down the hall by my wrist. "We'll call you if anything comes up. Good working with you!"

As soon as we were out of earshot, Rowan spun around to face me. I almost held my breath, waiting for him to start chastising me for my 'interpersonal differences' with Caledon. His wide-eyed expression suggested something entirely different was about to come out of his mouth, and my second instinct was right. He touched his hands to my biceps, nudging me so my back was to the wall and we were out of view from the bulk of the precinct.

"I know what we're dealing with," he whispered.

I blinked in surprise.

"You do? That's great!"

"No, not great. Definitely not great. Fairuz, it's Krampus."

"Krampus?" I frowned. I'd heard that name before. "You think evil Santa Claus ate our victim?"

A siren paused mid-step and gave me a funny look before continuing her way down the hall.

"Think about it, Fairuz. It makes sense. Problem kid disappears in the middle of the night, no signs of forced entry or anything, turns up half-eaten. You saw those bite marks. What else could do that?"

He had me with that last part. I had no idea what could have made those bites, *yet*. The rest had me shaking my head. I wasn't as familiar with European stories as I could have been, but I didn't think Krampus was responsible for eating our victim.

"I'm sure there's at least one other thing that could do that other than evil Santa Claus."

"Stop calling him that."

"He eats children at Christmas. What else do I call him?"

Rowan made a face. I made one back.

"Detectives?" Willoughby said, peering around the corner. "Another boy went missing last night. I don't know if it's related yet, but if you two would like to accompany me…"

"Is Caledon coming?" Rowan asked.

"There's no reason to believe it's a homicide yet, so—"

"We're in. You driving? Fairuz drives like an asshole."

I scoffed at that. I was an *effective* driver. He was just as bad, if not worse.

The new potential victim's house was walking distance from the first's. Having three detectives show up obviously worried the parents, despite our best efforts to assure them we were only being thorough and cautious. The new victim, Aiden Arak, was friends with Neil Greyson, and they'd gone missing within a week of each other.

"We thought they were together," his mother told Rowan

through tears. "We would have reported it sooner if we'd known— Goodness, poor Neil."

Neil's parents hadn't wasted any time sharing their son's fate. It twinged habitual suspicion inside me, but I brushed it aside. If the boys had been friends, it made sense that the Greysons would tell the Araks.

"He do this sort of thing often? Run away, I mean?" Rowan asked.

"Sometimes, he goes over to friends' and doesn't tell us, or comes home a few days later. I'm sure he's fine and you're wasting your time," Mr Arak said.

I let Rowan handle the conversation while Willoughby and I explored the room. This was my first time working a missing person case. Most of my career as a detective had been in the Homicide department, which meant I came in after the victims were found in less-than-ideal condition. I wasn't sure what I was supposed to be looking for.

The room could have been a mirror of my brothers' during their teen years. It was a mess, with posters all over the walls and clothes strewn all over the floor. How was I supposed to tell what didn't belong when nothing looked like it belonged?

"Arshad, look at this?"

I was glad I had Willoughby helping out. I moved over to him and crouched down to see what he was looking at.

"Dirt?"

Was that so unusual? The room was messy enough, I could imagine Aiden was the type to wear shoes inside. Looking around, I noticed it was the only clump of dirt in the room.

"What does it smell like to you?" Willoughby asked.

I looked up at him, unsure if he was joking or not. His expression suggested he wasn't.

"I don't smell very well," I admitted. "What is it supposed to smell like?"

"It smells like grave dirt to me."

I didn't want to ask how he knew what grave dirt smelled like.

"What does grave dirt have to do with Evil Santa Claus?"

I hadn't meant to say it out loud, and certainly not like that. My face flushed and I turned back to see if Mr and Ms Arak were still in the room. They weren't, thank *Allah*.

"Evil Santa Claus?" Willoughby repeated.

"Krampus," Rowan said, appearing behind me.

I jumped a little, catching myself before falling flat onto my face. Where had he come from? I stood upright, straightening my jacket in the process.

Willoughby was polite enough to cough over his laugh. "You think Krampus is responsible?"

"Make fun all you want, but it checks out."

"Then you know what the dirt is about?"

Rowan opened his mouth to answer, then shut it and narrowed his eyes. It seemed none of us knew what it was about. It gave me a bad feeling.

"We have to assume he's still alive," I said. "We need to figure out where this dirt came from, and fast."

Neil Greyson had been missing over a week before his body was found. Aiden Arak had already been gone three days. If the same person took them both, then we were running out of time.

Chapter 3

"What do you think I should get Ariadne for Christmas?" I asked.

I'd been staring at the same files for nearly an hour, and I was starting to go cross-eyed. My brain needed a break to reset itself.

The back corner of the second floor was quiet. Our team's other half were tracking down suspects in a burglary involving some high-powered wards. In the office behind me, Staff Sergeant Sabine Beaupré had finally taken a break from weekly argument with Inspector Vance. The only consistent sound came from the printer still stained with black ink.

I'd never been very good at buying planned gifts for people. If I spontaneously saw something I thought somebody would like, it wasn't a problem. The problem was that as soon as I actually had an occasion to buy for, my mind went blank. It was something about the pressure of buying the perfect birthday or Christmas gift that got to me. Random Tuesday afternoon just-because gifts had no expectations.

Rowan didn't miss a beat.

"Lingerie."

I rolled my eyes.

"Why do straight men always say lingerie? Does she seem like she'd be wearing that sort of thing?"

Rowan shrugged a shoulder and took a sip from his coffee.

"You got it backwards," he explained. "If she wears it, it's a gift for you. You have to buy *yourself* lingerie and wear it for her."

I crumpled up a piece of scrap paper and tossed it at him. It missed him and hit the cubicle wall behind him.

"Is that what you do for *your* girlfriends?"

"Hey, I used to look great in that shit. I can't rock a skimpy bra the way I used to since I got top surgery, though." He sighed dramatically and shook his head in mock mournfulness. "I don't miss it at all."

"You're an idiot."

He rolled his eyes, even though the corner of his lip was slightly upturned. "Speaking of which, I been doing some research on our missing teenager case."

Technically, we weren't involved in the other cases, only the one with a body. I didn't want to run with the assumption all these disappearances were connected. If they weren't, it was valuable time wasted. In a city the size of Toronto, it wasn't entirely impossible that it was a coincidence. Willoughby agreed, and was treating them as several different cases until a more concrete connection was found.

"What did you find?" I asked.

"Well, I didn't find anything referencing Krampus and grave dirt—"

"Shocking."

"— but he's still the only thing I found that makes a habit of stealing kids and eating them alive."

I drummed my pen against my desk. "These boys are a little old to be considered kids."

"Maybe. Four of these kids knew each other. Willoughby is still trying to connect the rest. They've all got histories of acting out. Theft, vandalism, drugs, breaking and entering. Total Krampus bait."

"Do we have any other theories? At all?"

Anything at all. Changelings, werewolves, a weird dog. I really wasn't sold on this Krampus idea. Rowan flopped through the pages on his file.

"Well… I also found our grave dirt connection. All these victims at some point or another got busted breaking into the cemetery."

"That grave dirt looked fresh."

"So either our victim's been there recently—"

"Or whoever took him was."

My own words made something click inside my head. Rowan must have seen the colour drain from my face, because he sat upright and straightened his beanie.

"I don't like that look. What's that look for?"

I bit the insides of my cheeks. My rings clicked against my desk as I drummed my fingers against it.

"Come on, Arshad. Last time you got that look, it was a fucking genie."

"Djinni."

"There's no *way* this can be worse than that."

That was at least true. It had been a hell of a first case with Special Crimes. I'd almost asked to transfer back to Homicide then and there. At least it had been our worst case so far. Nothing else came close to the unmitigated disaster that had been.

I let out a breath and scowled down at my keyboard as if I could force it to type out a better answer on my screen by sheer force of will. Nothing happened except Rowan kicking the leg of his desk.

"It sounds like it could be a ghoul."

Rowan stared and blinked slowly. Surely he'd heard of a ghoul. Everybody knew what a ghoul was. Children dressed up as them for Halloween.

"A ghoul," he repeated. "How does *that* make more sense than Krampus?"

Where did he want me to start?

"First of all, they're real. But they don't usually eat living victims."

"They don't usually live up here either, do they?"

I shrugged. "I actually hear some of them like the cold. It keeps bodies in eating condition longer."

Rowan rubbed a hand over his mouth. I wasn't sure if he was trying to resist the urge to be sick. He had only been sick once during a case and never since then, but part of me always expected him to puke at any bad body. While he'd seen some awful things in Sex Crimes, I, personally, didn't think it could have been as gruesome as what Homicide detectives saw. If I ever said it, he'd tease me for the Homicide ego.

"So we've got two theories. One is Krampus, who doesn't take teenagers. The other is a ghoul, which doesn't eat people alive. What does that leave us with?" Rowan asked.

My buzzing phone interrupted the conversation. It was a good thing, since I had no idea where that left us. Whichever one of us was right, we had two theories that only half-fit. Obviously, I thought I was right and I didn't think I was biased in it, either. There were many things out there that I didn't know about, but I really didn't think Krampus was one of those things.

The message was from Willoughby. My stomach dropped, and I sighed.

"It leaves us with another body."

Seventeen-year-old Mason Dover was the third boy to go missing, and the second to be found in the same place as Neil Greyson. There was more missing from him than from Neil. And like Neil, he had a criminal record. His most recent arrest was for trespassing in Prospect Cemetery.

"There's dirt under his nails," Deva said.

"Grave dirt," I said.

Rowan nodded, his usual scowl deepening into a frown.

There were plenty of ghouls back home. I used to see them all the time, especially when the violence got bad. Where there were bodies, there were ghouls to eat them. Sometimes, the unidentified and unclaimed ones would be left in piles where they lived. I was lucky enough to have spent most of my life away from the worst of it, but I never realized how strange it was to have ghouls roaming the streets until I moved to Canada.

Even back home, I never heard of one eating a living person. I supposed with all the fresh bodies, they didn't have to. Surely a ghoul would only resort to it if they were desperate. But even if that was the case, why not kill them first?

Whatever was going on, I didn't like it. From the look on Rowan's face, he didn't either.

"What are you thinking?" I asked.

It was a common question between the two of us.

Rowan asked out of what might have actually been respect. I asked because I was awful at reading faces at the best of times. With Rowan's even, neutral expressions, it was impossible.

"Something is off," he said. "This doesn't fit anything I know about."

"Not even Krampus?"

"Not even— Oh, fuck you. I don't think it's a ghoul, either. You said yourself, they don't eat living victims. That can't be sanitary."

"Neither is eating corpses."

Rowan covered his mouth with his hand. His eyes flickered to the trash can. It always felt bad how much I wanted to laugh when he got like this. He could make fun of me and my 'Homicide ego' all he wanted. At least I'd never gotten sick on a case. Half the detectives in Homicide had bets on how long it would take the squeamish detective to be sick. They'd also bet on how long it would be before I left. Nobody had guessed as high as three years.

"Do we have any other theories?" Rowan asked.

I shook my head. It was one or the other.

Rowan scratched his jaw. His eyebrows creased unevenly with his frown.

"There's a lot of things out there that fight with teeth. Ever seen what happens when a couple Old World sirens get into it? It sort of looks like this. But that rotting around the bites… I don't know, it's all weird."

"That's why it's a Special Crimes case," I said.

He tipped his head in silent concession.

"What's the game plan, then? I know two things about

ghouls. One is that they eat people, and the other is that I really don't want to deal with one."

I scratched my own jaw; then, realizing I was subconsciously mimicking him, pushed my hand through my hair. My rings caught in the obnoxious curls. He watched patiently with his eyebrows raised as I untangled myself. The autopsy continued around us. We might as well have not even been there for all Deva seemed to care.

"We'll go see where the bodies were left," I said, grunting as I ripped a few strands of hair from my scalp. "If a ghoul dumped them, there will be evidence."

"If there is?"

"Then we go to the cemetery."

"And if there isn't?"

I sighed. I appreciated that Rowan liked to work two steps in advance, but sometimes, it made these investigations so much longer than they had to be. If we found evidence of a ghoul at the dump site, it didn't matter what we would do if there wasn't.

"If there isn't, we revisit your Krampus theory."

"I know you're being sarcastic but I still say if it's not a ghoul, it's Krampus. Come on, Deva, you've got to have an opinion."

"My opinion," Deva said, "is that it isn't my job to give you opinions. My job is to give you facts."

As much as I loved Deva as a medical examiner, I had no idea how Ariadne could stand being her roommate. If I was her, I would move in with me just to get away from her. She might have been different outside of work. Who knew, she could have actually been *fun* when she wasn't examining the bowels of a half-eaten seventeen-year-old.

Rowan rolled his eyes. "I *guess*. Okay, let's go check out this dump site."

Chapter 4

The bodies had been left behind a dumpster near a food supplier. It was a short walk from Prospect Cemetery, and a reasonable drive from the Coroner's Complex. Rowan drove so I could flip through the case notes. It would have been easier to do with actual paper, but I had to settle with scrolling through my phone. My eyes ached from the strain. It was dry eyes, that was all. I didn't need glasses.

"Based on when our victims were taken and when they were found, the other missing boys might still be alive," I said.

Rowan only tapped the gas in response. When I looked up, his jaw was set hard and his ungloved hands gripped the steering wheel with enough force to turn their knuckles white.

"Rowan," I said softly, "you need to keep a level head."

He snorted, and his jaw loosened enough for him to say, "Big words, coming from you."

What was *that* supposed to mean? I was plenty level-headed. Before I could argue with him, we pulled into the parking lot of the food supplier. It was late enough in the day that Rowan's was the only car in the lot. We exited, and he locked the door manually.

"You should get the button replaced," I said.

"Should get the whole fucking car replaced. Next raise, I'm upgrading to something with a remote starter."

"Mine has that. It's amazing."

We circled the building. I caught Rowan's arm to stop him and pointed to the damaged police tape. It was probably nothing to worry about, but Rowan drew his gun and stepped behind me anyway. I exhaled slowly, focusing on the magic pooled beneath my skin. The burn started above my right hip and snaked its way up my body. The purple glow of Arabic calligraphy was hidden by my jacket and gloves. I pulled my right glove off on the off chance that I would have to throw up a barrier. I *could* do it through leather gloves, but it was much easier when I could actually touch it.

There was no sign of life around the dumpster. Most of the foraging animals were hibernating. I hoped they were somewhere warm. The magic beneath my skin wasn't enough to keep the chill from numbing my fingers.

The stench of the dumpster was enough to make me cover my nose with my arm. Three years of dealing with dead bodies plus a nose job made me fairly nose-blind, but this was bad.

"Footprints," Rowan said.

He pointed in my periphery. He was right. There were prints of bare feet in the thin layer of snow covering the ground. It had been snowing earlier; they must have been fresh. I crouched down to get a better look, careful to keep the edge of my jacket from touching the ground.

The feet weren't human. They were too long, the balls of the feet were too wide, and the scraped lines looked like claws.

"There's dirt in these tracks," I said.

"Aw, fuck."

"It isn't Christmas yet, you could still get your Krampus case."

"No, not that. Get over here."

I stood and met Rowan on the other side of the dumpster. It took me a moment to see what he was talking about, hidden beneath black garbage bags. My stomach twisted in a way that had nothing to do with the stench of rotting garbage, and everything to do with the fresh, half-eaten body beneath it.

"Deva says whatever was eating these victims, it was going between them," Rowan said, barely audible over the wailing siren.

Cars pulled over and stopped for us. This technically wasn't an appropriate use of sirens. They should have only been used when somebody was in immediate danger, but for all we knew, the fourth missing boy was running out of time. It was better to use them and not need them than to not use them and need them.

We made it to the cemetery in record time. Lonn O' Ceallaigh, the owner of the cemetery, met us at the gates, wringing his hands together nervously. His grey skin was clammy, and his eyes darted around nervously.

"Am I under arrest, officers?" he asked in a wheezy voice.

"That depends. What do you know about a ghoul hanging out in your cemetery?"

Lonn's eyes widened so far, I worried they were going to pop out of his skull. I didn't think I ever saw somebody missing their eyes before and I didn't want to.

"A ghoul? Goddess, no. One of the other cemeteries had one on their payroll, for people who want *alternatives* to burials."

Rowan held a hand up. "Back up. Are you saying that people *pay* to be eaten by a ghoul?"

"It's actually quite environmentally friendly. We don't offer that service here. I could get you their name if you'd like."

He flashed a nervous smile that showed short, flat teeth. Unless he had a second set of teeth like sirens, he certainly wasn't responsible for the bite marks on our victims.

"Please," I said. "That would be helpful. Would you mind if we took a look around?"

Lonn narrowed his eyes. "With a warrant, of course."

Rowan shot me a look.

"It's on its way," I assured.

While we waited for the police cruisers and search warrant, Rowan and I paced the perimeter of the cemetery. It might have looked like we were trying to intimidate Lonn, but the truth was, we were trying to keep warm without running the car. It got stuffy in there with the heat running.

"Think he's hiding something?" Rowan asked.

"It's hard to say. I think he was trying to protect himself."

"He was pretty quick to start pointing fingers."

I shrugged. Rowan tended to be paranoid, even by detective standards. Everybody always had an ulterior motive for everything.

"I wouldn't want to be responsible for this, either. He has more than himself to protect. He has a business."

Rowan said nothing. On the third lap around the cemetery, we slowed down to take in any details we might have missed the first two times. There wasn't much. It snowed on and off all week, which would have covered most of the older evidence.

"Hey." Rowan caught my arm. "Look at this."

This was a bend in the bars of the gate about the size of a trash can. The bars were embedded into the cold ground where they curved around a hole dug into it. He knelt on the snow to get a better look. I stayed upright where it was slightly warmer. He curled his hand over the hole and ran his fingers along it.

"That can't be how the boys got in. It's way too small," I said, even as I thought of Neil Greyson's broken bones.

"Suggesting there's something else getting in and out."

"A really big raccoon?" I asked hopefully.

Rowan snorted and shook his head. "I hope so, but I doubt it. "

"Does Krampus have claws?"

"You know what? I'm starting to think this might not be Krampus. Text Judge Fisher, see where that fucking warrant is."

Texting the judge took longer than it should have. Even with my gloves, my fingers were losing feeling. They really weren't as good as the purple ones I'd given Dasia. I missed them.

"It's waiting for us at the gates," I said when he replied.

There were many things I loved about Judge William

Fisher, but what I loved most was how quick he was to respond. He wasn't a man who wasted time, especially not where a missing person was concerned. It might not have been perfectly ethical to ask the judge married to my ex-fiancé for a warrant, but I only did it when it was *that urgent*. Considering there was still one missing boy who could have very well been somewhere inside this very cemetery, it was definitely *that urgent*.

We jogged back to the gates to find the uniformed officer holding a sealed envelope in her hand. I took it with only a curt thanks and passed it to Rowan. While I was pretty good at English, had an undergraduate degree in Criminology from the University of Toronto, and had been accepted to three separate law schools, I wasn't the fastest reader. Rowan could skim, I couldn't. I fixed my bulletproof vest over my jacket, and Rowan did the same.

"We're good to search the entire place as long as we don't do any damage or fuck up any graves. You guys hear that? No damage. We're looking for any sign of missing kids and a ghoul. If you see the ghoul, do *not* approach on your own. Radio for me or Detective Arshad. Preferably Detective Arshad, since this is her wheelhouse."

I almost made another Krampus joke, but the time for those jokes had passed. I was also too busy trying to figure out what a 'wheelhouse' was to come up with anything good.

Lonn only complained a little as he flipped through the warrant. He seemed to be reading it thoroughly, but his eyes weren't focused enough for me to believe it. I humored him for about twenty seconds.

"There is a missing boy. Whatever else is happening here, I promise you that's all we care about," I said.

His head snapped up to me. "Whatever else? Detective, there is *nothing else*. I am only concerned that you brutes will desecrate the dead."

I had been called a lot of things in my life and in my career, not all of them particularly flattering, but 'brute' was a new one.

"Lonn," I said, "we have given our team specific instructions not to upset anything. No harm will come to the bodies in your care."

His eyes softened slightly, and he pushed the warrant back into my hand. Scoffing, he disappeared toward his office.

"I'm taking that as the go-ahead. Smart, using his first name," Rowan said.

"I don't know how to pronounce his last name," I admitted.

Rowan only snorted before barking orders at the officers, telling them where to search. He and I walked toward the bent bars. If there was anything there to be afraid of, the cemetery was now crawling with officers. I wasn't worried. Rowan walked a few steps behind me with a hand on his gun. We had our vests, and I had my barriers.

Something about this place gave me a bad feeling, but I wasn't sure if it was because there was something odd here or because it was a cemetery. There was something about them that made me uneasy.

"Hey, Arshad. You believe in ghosts?"

"No." I paused. "A little bit."

I pushed the barrier into my hand to give me some light. Something moved. I spun, but I didn't see it. It was that big raccoon, I hoped, and nothing more.

"Toronto Police," I called anyway. "Come out with your hands up."

Shockingly, that didn't work. Of course it didn't, because the thing I'd seen was nothing more than a raccoon and I was scaring myself over nothing.

"Hey, Arshad. What do you call a can opener that doesn't work? A *can't* opener."

Either he was reading my nerves, or he was as nervous as I was.

Another shadow rushed past. I whirled around. The purple glow made Rowan's cheeks look hollow. His eyes were wide, and I really didn't like the way he was aiming his gun at my head.

"Rowan?"

"Don't move," he whispered. "Arshad, don't fucking move."

Oh, no.

His gun wasn't aimed at me. It was aimed at something behind me.

Chapter 5

There was a gun trained on a ghoul just behind my shoulder. So when Rowan told me not to move, I listened for once.

The ghoul must have been perched on the tombstone behind me. The direction of the wind changed, and the stench of rotting meat and old blood wafted over me. It was almost enough to make me gag. How hadn't I noticed that reek before? I knew my nose didn't work great, but even I should have noticed it. Rowan definitely should have, with his weak stomach for these sorts of smells.

"Come on, buddy. Let's not make this more difficult than it has to be," Rowan said.

"Difficult sounds fun." The ghoul's voice was deep and raspy, with no discernible accent.

"We want to talk to you," I said.

"I'm sure. You dicks do a lot of talking with your guns? Doing a little compensating for a *little* something down there?"

"Hey, fuck you," Rowan said. "You have teeth, I have a gun. I think that makes us even. Now why don't you step off there, and come with us so we can talk like reasonable adults."

"Who says I'm *reasonable*?"

Considering the ghoul was eating living people, I wouldn't have called him reasonable. Whatever purpose Rowan had for drawing out this conversation — maybe to get the ghoul to move enough to give him a clear shot or to draw the attention of nearby officers — it gave me time to figure out exactly where his head was relative to my elbow or the back of my head. Since my first case with Special Crimes, I'd taken up kickboxing. I wasn't the best fighter out there, but I had my white belt and I could hold my own during a spar. If I could knock him off the tombstone, it might stun him long enough for me to get my cuffs out of my back pocket and onto his wrists.

"Can I ask you a question?" I said.

"Oh, I'll tell *you* anything."

The obvious grin in his voice made me want to be sick more than the smell did. Since my back was to him, I didn't stop myself from rolling his eyes. Rowan's expression had gone into that patented stern blankness I hated. He was so good at keeping his face like that, I could never read what was going on inside his head. At least now I could make an educated guess.

"Since when do ghouls eat the living?"

Behind me, the ghoul laughed. It was going to take a lot of cleaning to get the smell of his breath out of my hair.

"Pretty recently, actually. These dumb kids kept breaking in here on dares. I might have scared one of them. He knocked his head pretty hard and I thought... Why not?"

"Why not," Rowan repeated dryly, his expression still unchanging.

"I tell you, you haven't *lived* until you've tasted raw, living human flesh. All that rich blood..."

He groaned next to my ear. I nearly shuddered. Rowan's lip twitched into a grimace for only a fraction of a second before he got it back under control.

"Sounds sanitary," he said.

The ghoul snorted. "You know how much bacteria is in dead things?"

Rowan tipped his head in a silent, *Yeah, I guess.*

The ghoul pulled my hair back and ran a clawed finger over the side of my neck.

"I'd love to take a big bite out of you."

This time, I did shudder. Then, I took a single step forward and threw my elbow into the ghoul's chest instead of his face. If I broke his nose, Sabine would never let me hear the end of it. The ghoul slipped off the tombstone, but it wasn't enough to completely knock him over. I whirled around in time to throw my hands over my face as he lunged at me.

My back hit the cold ground with enough force to knock the wind out of me. I gasped for breath. The weight of the ghoul settled on top of me kept me from being able to take a deep breath. A thin barrier wrapped reflexively around my arm, only just fast enough to protect me from the sharp teeth clamping down on it. Pain still bloomed through my skin. Clawed hands scraped at my shoulders through my jacket.

"Rowan!" I shouted. "A little help here!"

I managed to get enough leverage to slam my fist into the side of the ghoul's head. The leather covering my fingers wasn't enough to protect my knuckles. My gut knew before my brain that I'd done something wrong. The ghoul's head jerked to the side, and his teeth tore a hole in my jacket and the barrier. I slammed my knee up, but the ghoul shifted his weight to stop me from moving.

Rowan's gun was nowhere in sight when he ran in front of me. He threw his hands forward. His fingers extended into thin branches malleable enough to wrap around the ghoul's upper body. He pulled back, but the ghoul threw his weight down into me. The rotting meat smell of his breath made me dizzy.

The ghoul was now close enough to me that I could slam my forehead into his. White blinded me for a moment. The impact was enough to make the ghoul lurch back and give Rowan the leverage he needed to get him off me.

Slowly pushing myself to my feet, I took a mental inventory of any injuries. There were some scratches in my shoulder that would have to be cleaned. My skull throbbed from headbutting the ghoul. All in all, it wasn't bad. The ache in my fingers as I dug my handcuffs out of my pocket suggested I might have sprained them when I punched the ghoul. There was something satisfying about tightening the metal cuffs around his wrists.

The missing boy was found in one of the crypts. He was alive, but he didn't look good. The rotting around the bite marks had given way to infection. He'd lost a lot of blood, not to mention the massive chunks of muscle I didn't think would ever regrow. Even if he healed physically, he would never heal mentally.

The ghoul was Canadian-born, and had been living in the cemeteries of nearby Brampton until a few months ago, when he'd relocated to Toronto.

"At least it wasn't Krampus," Rowan said.

The shadows under his eyes suggested it was as much of a comfort to him as it was to me. I only nodded. I had to be on the road in an hour to get to my parents' place before the storm.

"Are you sure you don't want to come over for Christmas? There's plenty of space and food."

We would have to make space, but the food thing was true. Even though only my older brother's wife celebrated it religiously, Christmas dinner was met with the same amount of food as the *iftar* that came at the end of each day during Ramadan. It was a holiday. That meant waking up at four in the morning to start cooking. In my case, it probably meant an all-nighter in the kitchen.

Rowan shook his head. "As much as I'd love to see what an Arabic Christmas dinner is like, I have to pass. I'm taking shifts at some of the shelters. Besides, somebody has to stick around and make sure this city stays in one piece."

"It's a big responsibility," I said.

He lets out the smallest laugh possible. From anyone else, it would sound fake.

"My dad's coming over from Calgary for a couple days, so don't spend your whole trip feeling bad for me."

"I'll bring back leftovers," I promised.

"You'd better. Get out of here, Fairuz. You've got a long drive. I'll handle the paperwork on the ghoul."

I hesitated. Paperwork was a not-so-secret hatred we both shared.

"Are you sure?" I asked.

"Consider it my Christmas present to you. Or belated Eid, whatever."

That reminded me. I opened the bottom drawer of my desk and carefully pulled out my gift to Rowan. I walked around my desk to place it on his. Music played from the bulky headphones hanging around his neck. It sounded like a heavy metal version of *Deck the Halls*. He looked it over with a raised eyebrow as if unsure what to make of the red ribbon wrapped around the small pot.

"What's this?" He asked.

"You've never seen a cactus?"

He smiled down at the plant.

"I love it. Now go so you can buy something sexy for your girlfriend."

I finished up what I'd been working on, then placed holiday cards on the desks beside ours and slipped one under Sabine's desk before leaving the precinct.

Between the snow and traffic, what should have taken four and a half hours took six. I spent most of the drive talking to Ariadne on the phone.

My parents' small home in Ottawa was packed. My brothers and their families had already arrived, Emad from Boston and Amin from Thunder Bay. My cousin Imaan would be coming from Sudbury on Christmas Eve like Ariadne.

The days leading up to their arrival were chaos. Between taking care of my many nieces and nephews, keeping the house in one piece, and cooking, it was a relief when Christmas dinner was over. Mama bullied the men into doing the dishes, since the women had done all the cooking. Their complaints were good-natured, and it left us to talk over the *baklawa* and *halawat al-jibn* Imaan had brought, and the carrot cake Emad's wife Lacie made. It seemed she'd learned from last year, when her coffee-less coffee cake sparked a three day argument over what constituted coffee cake.

My family, with the notable exception of Emad, agreed it was cake with coffee in it. Lacie and Ariadne insisted it was cake to be eaten with coffee, which was ridiculous. All cake was eaten with coffee. It was late, though, so we were drinking cardamom chai instead, which might have been more caffeinated than coffee. The pot didn't stay full long, and we alternated filling it.

When it was Ariadne's turn, Imaan leaned over and smacked my thigh.

"When are you going to marry that girl already?" she whispered in Arabic.

I shushed her.

"What? It's not like she speaks that much Lebanese."

It was true. She'd been learning, but we still spoke English at home.

"We're not there yet," I said sharply.

"You left Homicide for her. You loved Homicide. Not in a murder way, but— You know what I mean. You loved the work."

"I love her more."

"Exactly! Tell her, Auntie."

Mama held her hands up and shook her head. The bangles on her wrist jingled.

"Oh, no. I'm banned from asking about marriage or grand babies."

As if that had ever stopped her before. It wasn't as though she didn't have enough grandchildren with the lovable hoard Emad and Amin had brought with them.

"Who's getting married?" Ariadne asked as she returned from the kitchen.

"My cousin," Lacey said quickly, cementing herself as my favourite sister-in-law over Rima this year.

"Oh, tell them congratulations."

I gave Lacey an appreciative smile. We finished the new pot of tea, which wasn't quite as good as the tea Dad made, before retiring to bed one by one.

Ariadne and I were on an air mattress in the living room. It felt only right to let the kids have the bedrooms. My brothers and sisters-in-law had the basement room to share, giving us the most privacy. I wasn't thinking of doing anything in my parents' house, especially with my entire immediate family under one roof, but if she wanted to, it was an option.

She rarely did want to, and that was fine with me. It was more intimate to let her brush my hair and weave it into a tight braid. I didn't have full range of motion in my right shoulder, which sometimes made it difficult to do myself. When she was done, she trailed her hands over my bare shoulders, only interrupted by my bra. Her fingers smoothed over the tattoos on my shoulder blades. The sensation disappeared over the scar covered by a cedar tree.

"I got you something," she said quietly.

It wasn't quite a whisper, but it still made me remember Rowan's lingerie suggestion. Surely she wouldn't bring that to my *parents'* house.

"Me first," I said.

I pulled my nightshirt on and rummaged through the purse beside me until my fingers found the small, white box. The light filtering in through the curtains was enough to make the pendant my parents got her that spelled out her name in Arabic shine. Her eyes shone, too. I slipped the box into her hand. Sweat broke out across my lower back.

"It isn't jewelry," I promised.

She was too practical for that. Her fingers pried the lid off, and she smiled brightly at the glossy pen and matching stand.

"It's beautiful," she breathed.

Relief brought a smile of its own to my lips.

"It's charmed, too. It'll always go back to the stand. Don't worry, I got it on sale."

I didn't, but she didn't need to know that. She brushed her fingers across my jaw and ran her nose along mine, but she didn't quite kiss me. It almost hurt.

"I love it."

She leaned across from me, giving me a view of the bird tattooed on the back of her neck. I almost ran my fingers over the wide-spread wings.

The box she handed me was small, definitely a jewelry box. My heart raced. I swallowed down the anticipation and opened it.

It wasn't a ring, but a pair of sterling silver earrings. At the bottom of each sat an amethyst stone about the size of my pinky nail. I'd seen them in the store a few times, and I knew exactly how much they cost. I swallowed down the lump in my throat.

"I'm sorry. I— I thought you'd like them. The part that goes into your ear is stainless steel, so you won't react to them. I can return them if you—"

"What? No!" I clutched the box protectively to my chest. "I love them. I— love you."

I'd said it before. It shouldn't have been as scary as it was. We'd been together for three years now. The ghoul hadn't bothered me, but *this* did?

This time, she tipped her head up and kissed me. Fireworks danced behind my eyelids. She pulled away before anybody could catch us, or before I could get any ideas. Short as it was, it left me dizzy.

"Merry Christmas, Fairuz."

"Merry Christmas."

The End

7

JÓLAKÖTTURINN

CHARLES REIS

*K*atrin stood next to a gas lamppost in the market area in Reykjavík, Iceland. The thirteen-year-old shivered in her old, unkempt clothes while her sheep skin shoes rested in an inch of snow. A dirty cap stretched down her head and over her ears with some long blonde hair sticking out from under it. She held a small metal cup while singing *Ó, helga nótt*, "Oh, Holy Night". With boisterous enthusiasm, she raised her voice over the sounds of horses wailing, wagon wheels rumbling on the cobblestone road, and the crowds of people talking.

An older man walked by, dropping a coin in her cup and then tipping his hat. She nodded and said *Gleðileg jól*, "Merry Christmas", as he entered a tavern with a gambrel roof. When he opened the door, the roars of men spilled out into the street. Since her mother, her Mamma, died last May, she became a daily fixture here. The holiday season made the patrons very generous. A faint smile crept on her face as she shook the cup and listened to the rattling of the coins. She guessed she had over 140 krona.

A black cat dashed from behind a nearby wooden barrel, stepping in the snow while it wiggled its nose. It approached the girl, stopping a few feet from her to look up with its yellow eyes. Katrin took a step back, staring at the creature. The hair bristled on her neck while her stomach fluttered. The cat meowed; Katrin shrieked and kicked snow at the animal. As she watched the feline jolt across the street, she breathed a sigh of relief.

Her twin brother, Halldor, emerged from an alley across the street. A blue scarf wrapped around his neck - a gift from their mother last Christmas - made it easy to spot him in the crowd. He rushed to his sister, pushing his way past several people. Huffing and puffing, the husky boy stood in front of her with a large grin. He told her that he got them permanent work on a sheep farm in Selfoss. The excitement in his voice increased when he said they wouldn't have to beg anymore.

A sparkle formed in her blue eyes. While bouncing in place, she held up the cup. To honor what their mother taught them, Katrin wanted to buy them new clothes and have one last Christmas Eve dinner in the city.

Halldor shook his head. *"Nei."* He insisted they had to leave as soon as possible. Along with having no time for such a celebration, they had to use the money for the trip.

Katrin frowned; disappointment etched into her face with tight lips and focused eyes. Since their father died when they were infants, Mamma struggled to earn money working as a seamstress. Although they remained in poverty, every holiday she worked extra hard so her children could have roasted lamb for dinner and new clothes to wear for the holiday. It tired and stressed her, but she did it without complaining.

She remembered what happened last year. The fireplace roared as she approached Mamma, who sat in her rocking chair while sewing a blanket. With tears in her eyes, Katrin told her to use the extra money to pay off debt instead of buying clothes for the siblings. Her mother smiled and tapped her daughter on the cheek. Mamma said it was important that she made sure her children have new clothes for Christmas Eve.

While Katrin admired her mother's giving nature, she hated the suffering she went through. She tilted her head and asked why.

Mamma looked down at her sewing needles and said, "Jólakötturinn."

Goosebumps covered her flesh. The idea of that creature had been installed into her psyche, giving her nightmares and hatred of cats. Jólakötturinn. The Christmas Terror. The Yule Cat. The Giant Man-Eating Beast. It roamed the country on Christmas Eve, searching out those who didn't have new clothes. The monstrous cat devoured these people, even if the reason they had no new outfits was from poverty rather than laziness.

Katrin quivered with fear as she looked down at the floor. Mamma smiled, telling her never to worry. She would make sure they were safe from the monster. The fire warmed their skin as they hugged. That holiday went off with plenty of joy and happiness.

But Mamma was no longer there to make sure they were

safe. The pain of her death lingered in her heart like a broken blade. Frustration slammed into Katrin as she balled her hands. With that memory fresh in her thoughts, she chastised Halldor for ignoring what their mother taught them. The cracking of her voice accompanied her pleas that they had to do something to appease the creature, or they wouldn't survive the night. Tears fell down her cheek.

Halldor shook his head, explaining that while he believed in the Yule Cat, they needed the money to pay their way to Selfoss. He crossed his arms and locked eyes with his sister. Katrin placed her hand that held the cup behind her back and scrunched her face. Her anger warmed up her face as she raised her voice, refusing to go anywhere.

Neither moved or said a word for over a minute. Eventually, Halldor sighed and uncrossed his arms. He told her that she was stubborn like Mamma. Katrin proudly nodded over that similarity.

With his eyes focused on the ground, he scratched his chin. After a few moments, he perked up to suggest that they give money that remained from hiring the driver to their church. Since their entire family were devoted Lutherans, he believed that would please Jólakötturinn. He placed his hand on her shoulder, telling her to trust him on this.

Since the death of their Pabbi, Halldor took over the responsibilities of their father. Katrin stood there motionless, processing his proposal. She went back and forth between what to do. While looking up at the sky, she thought about their parents staring down from Heaven. Mamma would insist they get new clothes as the tradition demanded, but Pabbi would approve of Halldor's plan.

She asked him if he was sure that would work. With a smile on his face, he hugged her and spoke into her ear, affirming he would never let any harm come to them. After letting go, she playfully tapped his cheek and handed him the cup. She straightened his scarf and affirmed he trusted him. God would look out for them, she said. Their luck was ready to change.

The black cat returned, rubbing against Halldor's legs. Her brother knelt to pet it. It purred while he scratched its head. With her heart pumping, Katrin closed her eyes and took a step back. With each breath she took, she tried to beat down her fears. Her eyes flung open when she felt Halldor's hand on her shoulder. He giggled, telling her that this cat was too small to be Jólakötturinn.

Nightfall. The moon rested high above. The siblings' hired driver dropped them off at a country crossroad a few miles from Selfoss. It was as close as he could get without deviating too much on his own travel. After wishing the man a Merry Christmas, the two started the one-hour journey to their new home.

For the past thirty minutes, they walked down a snow-covered road that cut through a forest of birch and aspen trees. They hadn't seen a person since the driver, nor come across any building or animal. The sounds of their breaths and the gentle wind rustling the branches accompanied them on this isolated hike. When she saw her brother's dirt-covered clothes and scarf, along with her own scruffy clothes, she wished they bought new ones. However, she took comfort in knowing their church would use the money from them to help the poor.

The heavy rucksacks filled with supplies that they carried on their backs slowed them down. Katrin walked several feet behind her brother. With each step taken, she slouched her back while her hands gripped the straps. The cold tickled her skin. Even as her muscles ached, she maintained a positive attitude.

Hægðu á þér, "Slow down," Katrin said with broken breaths. Although she would miss Reykjavík, she knew a better life existed in Selfoss, making the discomfort worth the price. She just wanted to get there without collapsing from exhaustion.

Halldor stopped and turned to her. With a devilish smirk, he teased her that she was always the slow one, which was why he was born first. He laughed. She grinned, taunting him that while he had the speed, she got the brains. His eyes and mouth opened in an amusing surprise. He took off the rucksack and dropped it. Halldor bent down and grabbed a handful of snow, molding it into a ball. Cheerfully, he said he would get her for that.

After dropping her rucksack, Katrin giggled and picked up snow. The race to strike first ended with Halldor throwing his snowball, striking her in the chest. She instantly responded by tossing her ball with a grunt. It slammed into his shoulder, splattering into pieces. The kids laughed and created more snowballs. Projectiles flew through the air in their mini-war filled with laughter and joy. Despite her muscles being sore, Katrin loved every minute of their playtime.

A snapping noise from the distance froze her in place. A

snowball slammed in her face, but she didn't react. Instead, she stared into the forest as a cold chill crept down her spine. Shivers raged through her body and her stomach fluttered. She knew something watched them, cloaked in the darkness. Many times, she traveled into dark woodlands where the most dangerous animal was an Arctic fox, but never sensed danger before. Tonight, she felt different.

Er allt í lagi?, "Are you okay?" Halldor said. She shushed him and told him to listen. They stood there, motionless. She squinted her eyes to see anything that might reside in the pitch black that existed beyond the visible trees. The wind increased, trees danced around, and misty snow glided along the ground, but nothing else was seen.

A louder snap came from the same direction. The siblings gasped and jerked back. Katrin grabbed her brother's arm with her trembling hand, digging her fingers into him as her skin tingled. Although nothing was visible, she knew something stalked them. Despite the cold, she felt hot and sweat formed on her face. She wanted to run but remained incapable of moving.

A third snap happened closer than the last. Halldor, in a shaky voice, said it was likely a reindeer. His body quivered and he hardly blinked. Knowing that fear overcame the bravest boy she knew increased her own.

The darkness revealed its truth. Two red eyes larger than any wagon wheel glowed several yards away. Black vertical slit pupils cut through the center. The eyes stared at the children, glistening brighter with each passing second. The rest of the creature remained cloaked in the shadow.

Katrin compressed her lips as she took a step back. Her

screams refused to surface. Gasping and wheezing, her breathing acted as if someone choked her. As she took more steps back, she pulled Halldor along, who remained stiff with terror.

An ear-piercing screech erupted from the position of the eyes, slicing through the air before cutting into the siblings' ears. They screamed and covered their ears. Katrin recognized the sound as belonging to a cat, but a far bigger one. No doubt, Jólakötturinn arrived. They broke free of their paralyzing fear and ran for their lives. Katrin led the way, sprinting in the opposite direction of the creature.

She raced through the forest. Her legs burned. She kicked up snow as her clothes flowed in the wind. Steam rapidly spewed from her mouth. Moonlight provided some help as she dodged trees and hopped over stumps. The snapping of branches and cracking of trees resonated from behind. Loud thumps and the rumbling of the ground boost her adrenaline.

She jerked her head around. "*Halldor!*"

He dashed forward, his scarf swinging in the air. Sweat poured down his blemished face. *Hlaupa! Hlaupa!* "Run! Run!" Halldor said while waving his hand forward. The red eyes followed a few yards behind him.

She ran. Freezing air entered her lungs. The terror that infected her mind removed any sense of time. She slipped and stumbled to the ground; her face splattered into a foot of snow. Halldor grabbed her arm and yanked her up. A sharp pain throbbed in her shoulder as she got back on her feet. Halldor pointed to a group of large, monolith shaped rocks several yards away. They held hands and raced towards them.

They crouched behind the rocks, which shaded them in darkness. Katrin's chest rapidly rose up and down while the sounds of her heartbeat battered her ears. Halldor placed his arm over her back, so she leaned against him.

Heavy stomps rumbled the ground like an approaching thunderstorm. A tree crashed to the ground to the right. A massive shadow encroached over the spot; it had long, pointed ears and a large, oval-shaped head that moved back and forth, exposing its box-like snout. Katrin covered her mouth while sweat poured into her eyes, stinging them.

A hiss resonated in the air. A cackle accompanied the shadow's movement leftward and vanished from their view. The drumming of stomps and tremors played out from a few feet away. The creature remained near but out of sight. She grabbed her brother's arm, squeezing it so hard that her fingers ached. Never did she imagine that her worst nightmare would turn into reality.

Halldor whispered a plan into her ear. He would have the cat chase him, allowing her to escape. While holding her hand, he reminded her that he was a fast runner and would easily outrun it. She shook her head and begged him not to do it. The situation was dire, but they were in this together.

His lips trembled; he reached into his pocket and pulled out a small brown bag. When Katrin realized it was filled with coins, her mouth burst open. A glint of tears formed in her eyes as she looked into his own. The shock prevented her from uttering *Af hverju?*, "Why?", but instead she lipped it out in a silent whisper.

He looked down and said *Fyrirgefðu mér*, "Forgive me", explaining that after he left her back in the city, he didn't give the money away. Instead, he planned to save it in a bank near their new home for both of them. There was no other way, he reasoned, for he had to do this as repentance for betraying her trust.

With tremors raging nearby, she grabbed then tossed the money bag into the snow. She tightened his scarf while looking directly into his eyes. As her heart pounded and eyes twitched, she forgave him. Money meant nothing to her, but life without him would be one of misery. By God's grace, she believed, they both would make it through the night. Katrin told him to run as if he was trying to catch a reindeer.

She said *Ég elska þig*, "I love you", and Halldor replied the same back. Katrin gripped her hands and prayed for protection for them both.

Once Halldor pumped up his chest, he jumped to his feet and rushed towards some thick woods. Several feet from the rocks, he waved his arms while calling out to the creature as he ran.

A blaring screech erupted. Katrin covered her ears while watching her brother run like a rabbit escaping a fox. Small quakes followed as the cat, taller than any building she saw back home, pounced for Halldor. The moonlight illuminated its ruffled black fur. Its thick legs slammed into the snow and its lengthy tail snapped a birch tree in half, sending the top portion tumbling to the ground. Halldor endured with his calling as he entered the woods. The creature followed; it didn't take long for the darkness to swallow them up.

Fear swirled in her mind over the possibility of death. She sprinted in the opposite direction as adrenaline flowed through every portion of her body. The wind slammed against her face and the forest appeared blurry.

She had no idea how long she ran before spotting lights shined in the distance like twinkling stars. Blocking out the world to focus on the light, she pushed her legs harder and concentrated on her speed. With steady breathing and pounding heart, she rushed towards it.

A small house emerged from the darkness. On the wooden front façade, lights flickered from a square window on each side of the door. The slanted, green turf roof stretched to the ground. Katrin sprinted for the building, hoping this would be her salvation.

She pounded her fist on the door, rattling it with each blow. *Hjálp! Hjálp!*, "Help! Help!", she cried out. After a few seconds, the door creaked open. An older man with gray hair and a beard peeked out. He asked what he could do for her, but she pushed open the door and barged past the man.

She entered a small room illuminated by the fire in the brick kitchen fireplace. On its mantle laid a triangle-shaped candelabra with seven lit candles. Katrin moved next to a square wooden table with small bowls filled with rice pudding and dishes loaded with ham, potatoes, and cabbage. A gray-haired woman wearing a long black skirt, jacket, and tail cap stood nearby. Katrin assumed she was the man's wife. The husband closed the door, then asked the girl if she needed help.

Meow. Under the table, a gray kitten sat up straight while looking up, moving its tail. *Meow.* It tilted its head as it purred while reaching up with a paw. With horror creeping into her, Katrin screamed. She stumbled backward and fell into the grasp of the husband. The cat hissed and ran into another room, vanishing from her sight.

As Katrin screamed and tears rolled down her cheeks, the wife grabbed a blanket. She placed it over the girl's shoulders and then guided her to sit in a rocking chair. On a nearby counter rested a water-filled metal basin. After grabbing a small cloth and soaking it in the basin, the wife washed the girl's face. In a soft voice, she asked what happened.

While shaking uncontrollably, Katrin stuttered the word, "Jólakötturinn."

A glowing eye peeked through the front window. It blazed like burning wood and its vertical slit pupil moved side to side until it focused on Katrin like a hawk on a field mouse. With a chill vibrating through her body, she sprinted into a corner and sat into a fetal position, crying. The husband and wife ran to each other and embraced.

The eye moved out of sight. An intense screech cut through the air. Heavy thumps rattled the wall while the cat circled around the home. With each thump, the noise and rattles grew louder. Then they stopped. An eerie calm overtook the dwelling, with only the sound of a crackling fire to accompany them.

Katrin held her breath and her heart slammed against her rib cage as she looked around the home. Seconds passed, yet the silence remained. After breathing a sigh of relief, she thanked God for sending the creature away.

A boisterous thud slammed against the side of the house. The structure shook. Dust plunged from the ceiling, cups tipped over, and picture frames crashed to the floor. Katrin covered her ears and screamed. Another bump hit the house and a short quake rumbled the walls. More items crashed to the floor.

The woman turned to her husband, telling him to get the other outfit he made for her. He nodded and rushed through a doorway that led to the back of the home. The wife approached Katrin and grabbed the wet cloth. With gentle strokes, she wiped the rest of the smut off the girl's face.

Her muscles tensed up, but Katrin didn't twitch as the woman cleaned her cheeks. While the wife explained what must be done to appease the creature, Katrin focused on her mother, wishing she followed Mamma's teachings. The regret of not following the proper protocol scrambled her emotions. Fear. Doubt. Regret. Disbelief. It all flowed through her mind, knocking into each other.

The husband returned with clothes in his hand, and the wife took them. The next several minutes were a blur. When her mind refocused and her sense of time returned, Katrin found herself standing in front of the door. Upon looking down, she discovered that she wore a long, green wool skirt with a matching jacket and black tail cap. The wife straightened the clothing while she explained that the Yule Cat would tear down the house at any moment. Christmas Day was hours away, so they couldn't wait it out. Katrin had to stop it by going outside to show it the new clothes.

Although fear cursed her like a plague, the girl wanted to protect the couple. While they followed the rules, the cat would destroy their home and kill them in the process to get to her. She knew Mamma would have encouraged her to do it. As the door opened and freezing air rushed in, she prayed that all the tales about the Jólakötturinn were true. After a deep inhale and exhale, she stepped outside.

A geyser of mist erupted from her mouth and the cold struck her skin. She swallowed to clear up the saliva that grew in her throat. Her arms and legs quivered. The girl took six steps away from the door while the couple stood by the entrance with bowed heads and hands held in prayer.

Katrin looked right and slowly panned the landscape. The trees danced as the wind whipped through them. Creaking branches and whooshing wind harmonized together. The moonlight shined on top of the trees and the snowy field that surrounded the house. Several large paw prints were scattered throughout the area, but she didn't see the creature.

A deep, raspy hum loomed from the left. With her eyes unable to blink, she slowly glanced over. Jólakötturinn stood on its legs with its tail erect, towering over the house. Its chest rose and decompressed. Its whiskers twitched and its upper thin lips curled to expose fangs. While maintaining its stare at the girl, it stomped in closer. A small quake vibrated the ground.

Paralyzed with fear, Katrin stood in place and controlled her urge to vomit. Sweat covered her face. Her breathing broke into a short gasp. Dizziness settled in. She struggled to prevent the erosion of what little bravery she had remaining. She imagined her mother stood behind her to pray for her daughter's survival with Halldor by her side so they could face this together.

The cat crouched down and sniffed the girl, starting from her legs and working its way up. A pungent, heavy odor of rotting meat secreted from it. Its snout twitched and nostrils expanded with each sniff. When its nose reached her face, warm mucus spread on to her cheek. Its breath warmed her skin.

Katrin pressed her mouth shut and held her breath, pressing her fingers into her palm. Her heart pulsated, feeling each forceful pump. She didn't know how much longer she could withstand this, so she prayed for God to end it.

Jólakötturinn stood upright. It wiggled its whiskers and purred. Then the creature licked its lips, turned, and walked away. Soft thumps mildly shook the ground. With each step, it grew smaller and the thumps softened. It uttered a meow that echoed into her ears. As it entered the forest, the trees encased it and it vanished into the darkness.

Katrin let out a deep exhale and collapsed to her knees. She couldn't believe this plan worked and that she survived. Calm overtook her soul. She clapped her hands and gave silent thanks to God. The couple joined her and shouted out in praise.

But gloom overtook her sense of happiness. On the side of the house where the cat once stood, a blue scarf laid in the snow. Katrin jumped off the ground and ran to it, whimpering like a scared puppy. She picked it up. Her knuckles turned white as she gripped it. Blood covered half of the scarf.

Loud screams burned her throat as she cried out Halldor's name. She pressed the scarf close to her face and fell to her knees again. The reality that Jólakötturinn killed him filled her with so much sorrow that she thought her heart and lungs would collapse. Her father, her mother, and now her brother resided in Heaven, leaving her alone in this cruel world.

The couple knelt beside her, wrapping their arms around her body. Katrin laid her head on the woman's chest. She coughed and gasped for air. Her hands shook. Goo dripped from her nose. Guilt over saving herself and the couple but not Halldor filled her heart. As tears cascaded over her face, she wished Jólakötturinn claimed her too.

-END-

8

THE WITCH OF WATER STREET

JON TOBEY

*T*hayer unfolded the wheelchair and reached into the car for little Sarah. Tim was already opening the door. Thayer smiled up at Brenda, his bride. "It's okay, Brin, go inside, I've got her." Tim was his son from his first marriage, Sarah came along with Brenda. Thayer saw no difference, though, and doted on her.

"Thayer, you own the oldest, most successful shipping company in Boston. You could afford a much nicer vacation home than this hovel. Why do we have to come here?"

Thayer sighed, reaching into the car to get Sarah's wheelchair. *Here we go again.* He stood up to say something, smacking his head on the roof of the SUV, wincing and barely containing a string of oaths. Sarah put her hand on his arm. "It's okay, Dad, I don't need it."

He smiled at her and rubbed her on the head while simultaneously rubbing his own "You run inside." Well, maybe *run* wasn't the right word, but Sarah was thwarting her diagnosis, and instead of her condition getting worse, it was getting better. He turned to his wife. "Brin, this is not a 'vacation home.' It's the familial homestead. My forefather, the founder of Piscataqua Enterprises, built this house with his own hands, every drawknife cut and hand-hewn peg, just like he built his first gundalow. Coming here, is coming home, to my – our – roots. It's an homage. It's okay to appreciate where we are, but it's not okay to forget where we came from.

"Besides, the kids love it here." He reached out and brushed snow off of her collar. "I wish you could learn to appreciate it just a bit."

"It's just so old, so cramped, so…."

"Historical." He swept his arm up the street to the city at his back. "The last wooden structure in all of downtown. The only one to survive the Christmas fires of 1653, 1779, and 1908."

"So, we visit during the most probable time for tragedy." She made a moue, but the situation was momentarily diffused.

For the rest of the afternoon, the house was a bustle of activity. Brin and the kids unpacked, Thayer hauled in the tree and stood it up in the corner and then went to the attic. He walked the length of the house, putting his hands on the joists as he went along to keep from banging his head, finally stopping in the cold and the dust. He smiled and patted the beam he held, hand-hewn, still with bark on it in places. It was a veritable master class in Yankee thrift, only straight and square at the end where its tenon pierced a rafter and was pinned with a carved peg. He smiled, and deep in his belly, something unwound. "Old girl, I missed you." Then he bent over to sort through the boxes and to retrieve the ancient iron base and blown-glass ornaments, some of them centuries old. Sighing once more, he went back downstairs to join the family.

While they decorated the tree, he started a fire, and segued into the kitchen to get dinner going. Roast goose with stuffing and fixings. Just getting a goose was a special order, even in Boston, but this had been the traditional meal as far back as he knew. Eventually, the rest of the family filtered in. Even though the kitchen was last updated in the 70s, it was still plenty capable of putting out a Christmas Eve dinner, especially if you knew how to use the fireplace and its warming ovens. It was even more special now that the kids were old enough to help. Little Sarah was so serious when she cut out the cookies, and Tim was proud that he was allowed to use one of the paring knives to help prep.

The kitchen had a table, but they ate in the formal dining room, which took up the whole left of the house. Wall sconces threw indirect light about the room. Just enough to dispel the gloom and make it cozy, where it could've otherwise been a bit creepy. When dinner was over, he looked across the table at Brenda, who looked more tired than replete. This was the furthest thing from the magazine-layout parties she favored, but he reveled in the rare alone time with just the four of them. Never in his 47 years had he missed Christmas in this house, and he never intended to.

"Another fantastic Christmas feast, eh gang!" He lifted his

cobalt blue, hand-blown wine glass to toast, as had his father and his father's father back a dozen generations and more, and the kids raised their eggnogs. They had to cajole their mom, but she eventually gave in. "Not everybody gets to toast Christmas with a century-old Burgundy. The least of many good reasons I'm glad my ancestors got into wine, and not the triangle trade. Merry Christmas to all."

"And confusion to our enemies," chimed Tim, who had once heard Thayer quote his own father.

Thayer smiled. "I think that toast has already come true."

After the toast Thayer announced, "Okay, help clean up and then we can do stockings." The kids took off like key-wound toys to take food and dirty dishes into the kitchen where Thayer promised he would take care of them. Brin was still downtrodden.

"What's the matter, hon?"

Brin looked around the candlelit room, it's low 350-year-old ceiling crossed by beams, the plaster casting the light softly back. "Couldn't we, just once, have Christmas in the city?"

He sighed. They were about to run a script, and he hated running scripts. They both knew exactly where this was going, their lines to the letter, and even the dramatic outcome, so why did she bother? Just then, the kids came charging back into the room. Sarah was using one crutch, but keeping up nevertheless. They grabbed their parents by the hands and dragged them into the parlor where a cheery fire burned in the shallow brick fireplace. Brin had filled the stockings while they were making dinner, and the little trinkets and toys, mere appetizers for the morning, were soon unwrapped and scattered about. Thayer looked at the family in front of the fire, and the feeling in his belly started to glow warmly. This was home. This was what it was all about. A happy family, a safe place. And this house, as stalwart and true as any servant could be. Once again, he reached out and touched it, the smooth wood of the wainscoting, gone dark with age and not stain, and marveled at the loving craftsmanship of the builder. Simple things, perfectly executed. It always centered him to be here.

Tim snapped him out of his reverie. "Tell us the story about the Christmas Witch! Please!"

Thayer smiled. Where some families might do *The Night Before Christmas* before sending the children to bed with sugar plum dreams, he spent his childhood in this very room listening to his father tell the story, and now he was passing it down to his kids.

Brin groaned aloud. "Do we have to? It's barbaric."

Thayer shrugged. "It's a tradition. I promised my father I would tell it, as he promised his father, and so on back to when this house was new."

She crossed her arms over her chest and kick-pointed out her feet in a mock Russian peasant dance singing, "Tradition!"

Well, he thought, at least she was capitulating with some humor. "Make all the fun you want, dear, every part of the legend has held true for going on four centuries, and I'm not about to break it." He went into the kitchen and gathered the things he'd already prepared onto a tray, pricking his finger with a pocketknife so the kids didn't have to see it. Although, Tim would probably be into it, he thought.

He brought it back and everybody took their place while he told the tale.

Coming back into the room with a brandy, he sat in a chair in front of the fire, the children at his feet, Brin to his left. "And so, children, let me tell you the story of the Witch of Water Street, and pay attention, for someday, this will be your tale to tell to your children, and you best get it right, or there will be hell to pay."

Ebidiah had been tracking the big buck since soon after daylight. He felt blessed. The stag would feed the settlement for the Yule feast and days after. The wind shifted to the northeast, blowing from him to the deer. Ebidiah had been waiting for this. He could never catch up to the stag, especially not in the snow. But the buck was king of the forest, he would want to know what sought him out and would circle around to see his pursuer. Experience told Ebidiah the deer knew by now it was being tracked, so he sat on a stump and unwrapped his breakfast of bread and cheese.

Ebidiah said Grace and crossed himself before he ate, looking around. He could see a long way between the bare trees, and it was absolutely silent. Not even a bird was chirping. The hunter felt a storm coming in his bones. Finishing his repast, he brushed the crumbs into the snow. A few flakes drifted down, and he picked up his rifle to head back whence he came.

At the top of a rise he found a good tree, wide enough to

hide his bulk, with a branch to hold the gun. Just behind it was a chair-sized granite boulder to rest on. Here is where he would wait for his quarry. The snow came thicker, lessening his sightlines, but he kept to his post. In the gray light, it was impossible to track the sun, but Ebidiah felt he still had time to shoot and skin the buck and pack it out before dark. He hoped he did because, despite its humble beginnings, he had a feeling this storm coming out of the North Atlantic would last for days and he wanted to be home by his hearth before it hit.

Patience, as the good Father Bennett oft counseled, was a virtue. But foolhardiness was a vice. It would not do to miss his shot, but it would be a greater loss to die in a storm. As he weighed these two ponderous truths, the buck materialized out of the snow, like a ghost condensing out of the night. He was much closer than Ebidiah thought he would be when he saw him, and Ebidiah raced to get the cover off his gun and position it.

When at last he sighted down the barrel, at first he could no longer see the deer. But then, there was motion among the trees and the stag rematerialized, blurry in the building storm. His antler rack was magnificent, how he moved through the woods was a wonder. The deer was almost upon him, and Ebidiah had far less time to set up and take the shot than he originally intended when he thought he would spot the beast coming over the rise.

"God has weighed my efforts and favors me," thought Ebidiah. The deer stopped, lifted its snout, and sniffed the breeze, turning its head slowly and looking directly at the hunter. For a moment, they looked each other in the eye, and

Ebidiah froze. Finally, he shook it off, and taking advantage of the stag's pause, took his shot.

At that moment, the branch broke, and already off balance from the recoil, Ebidiah slipped on the compact snow under his leather soles, fell backwards, and cracked his head on the granite he had been resting on. The deer jumped and was gone, dissolving into the storm as easily as if he were made of snowflakes.

Charis had also come out before dawn to take advantage of the calm before the storm. She carried a long piece of debarked black locust with a burl at one end, like a mace. In the bitter cold, swinging it at the low-hanging dead branches snapped them off with ease. Much faster and more reach than a saw. She collected as much as she could carry and now was trying to get out of the storm. She was making good time, her homemade snowshoes swinging wide under her cloak.

The shot startled her, breaking into her reverie. What damned fool would be out hunting in this weather? Couldn't he smell the Nor'Easter coming on? Suddenly the buck bounded past her, crashing out of one thicket, and heading past her into the next without notice. There was blood on the snow every few steps. She shuffled over to the spoor, and picking up the black blood on the tip of her finger, tasted it. She nodded and waved the cudgel at the departed deer. "Ah, good for you my friend. It's not heart blood. You'll live to see the Yule."

Charis leaned on her bat for a moment. She half-expected

some farmer to come barreling after, following the blood trail. When one did not, she scratched her head through her cap. It was no business of hers, surely. And, if she found the man, odds are he was daft and not hurt and he would shoot her thinking he had tracked his quarry in the storm. None of this rationalizing would demur her, though, she knew. She heaved a mighty sigh and adjusted the faggot on her back, then turned to follow the deer's tracks back whence they had come. The tracks were deep, and the blood was fresh, but the snow was intensifying. She had to hurry if she was not to lose the trail.

When she came to the valley, she stopped for a moment on the rise, looking for her hunter. Nothing stirred amongst the bare trunks. She descended into the vale, started up the other side, turned around, then turned around again. No. This was it. The deer walked to this spot. Stood here. Then took off running. There was no blood before this. Here was where the shot happened. She looked both ways. There on her right, very faint, but on the lee side of a maple, she saw the slash of a new wound, the bullet. She turned to the left, so somewhere along a line between that slash and through where she stood now, she would find the hunter's stand.

It figures, she thought, *that he would be uphill.* Sighing again, she began the climb. She found Ebidiah under a light dusting of snow, the snow beneath his head soaked in blood. She *tsked* as she bent down to inspect him.

"Damn fool. Always a damn fool," she muttered. And always her taking up the burden, making sure to get him back whole to his kinfolk. Begrudgingly, she undid her bundle of firewood and leaned it against the stub of the branch he had set the rifle on so she could find it again later. Then she began scouting around. Above her on the ridge she spotted some white pine and began trudging up the hill, powered by a steady stream of remonstrations against both the foolishness of the man behind her and her own damned goodwill. "No time to go back, gonna get caught out. Find you frozen out here like a statute."

She took off her snowshoes and crawled in under the snow-laden branches to be near the trunk, then reaching under her cloak she pulled a hatchet out of her belt. In short order she had two long branches cut. She put her shoes on and dragged the branches back to Ebidiah. Cutting strips from her skirt with her knife, she quickly laid the two branches out so that they crossed at the thick ends, then laid sticks from her bundle across it, creating a travois. She hauled the man onto it, looked at his rifle, sighed, put it in the covering and put it against the tree with her sticks. It was too heavy to add, and if they didn't get out of here, he wouldn't be needing it anyway.

Standing o n the narrow side of the X made by the branches, she used them as handles. Dragging the body behind, she skidded him back to the game trail on the valley floor and began a slow plod home. By the time she dragged him to the edge of the vale, her breath was coming hard and she was soaked. This, she knew, was the first step to death. She took off her cloak and tossed it over Ebidiah's inert form. "This now would be a good time to be jumping up, were you thinking you might be getting better sooner than later," said she. "And perhaps then be dragging me home before it's me who freezes to death out here." She expected no answer, and getting none, resumed her labors. Already, dark was coming upon them, and with it the storm had arrived true.

When she got to her own snowshoe-packed trail packed, it got somewhat easier. There are some things, the doing of which is unimaginable, unless the not doing is worse. Charis dragged and swore and panted and fell the man home in a struggle beyond comprehension. When they got to her log cabin, she dropped to her knees, undid her shoes, and checked Ebidiah to see if there was life enough in him to make it worth carrying him in. With the last of her strength, she dragged him across the threshold and kicked the door shut. She lay there on the floor with him, panting and spent, but the cold soon set into her bones and rattled them until she got up and put wood on the fire, tending it to a raging blaze.

"Now I know this is extravagant, especially as I swapped my bundle for your somewhat less useful carcass, but I'm in my only dress and I'm wet from the inside out. People would surely talk if I sat here nakid near the fire. So you will just have to wait until I can tend on you." With that, she fell asleep on the hearth.

The next day, she washed away the dried blood and probed his skull. Thankfully, it was not soft, the bones had not broken. She pried his eyelids open and studied the pupils. They were both pinpricks. He was still out, and his breathing was shallow, his pulse thready. She chewed the inside of her lip. He might never wake up, or he might wake up with a headache and be fine. Or, he might walk home and die in two weeks. Damn fool. She went to a cabinet and started pulling down herbs to make a potion to get the swelling down. Twice, she pulled down a bit brace and put it back. If there was bleeding on the brain, it would kill him eventually unless she drained it. If there wasn't, the drill hole could be worse than the original injury. The only way she could be certain is if she waited too long.

She sat him up by forcing her body in behind his on the hearth. She tilted his head back and spooned the powerful liquid into his mouth. After a time, he coughed and sputtered, let out a great sigh, and his breathing deepened.

"Ah, good work there, hunter, your soul almost escaped, but you caught it."

It went on like this for two days. The storm had settled into a steady light snow, but it was now halfway up the windows. The cabin was in a perpetual twilight. On the third day, she removed his clothes, bathed him, and put them in a kettle to boil. Then she took a knife and carefully scraped the hair off the skull around the wound. The flesh was purple, going to black. He groaned in pain.

"That settles it, me boy." She tied his hands and feet, pulled her skirts up to her waist, and tied them up to free her legs. She got the bit brace and put the tip in the fire. She rolled him over and sat on his back, then very carefully drilled a hole in his skull. She stopped when black blood began oozing out. She washed it carefully in boiled water until the water ran only the lightest pink and wrapped his head loosely with her finest linen.

With his clothes hanging before the fire stoked with the last of her wood, she opened the door, which sensibly swung inward so she could get out after a big snow. Wood was critically low, and it was time to go retrieve her faggot. With her snowshoes on, she had to half crawl, half swim until she got to the surface of the snow. Then she began a slow and steady trundle back where she found him. Even with the snowshoes it was tough going in the deep, light snow. *It's not as hard as hauling a pilgrim,* she reminded herself. She actually enjoyed being out in the fresh air after the stuffy cabin. When she got to the tree, she shouldered the firewood, and then looked over at the gun, still leaning there, covered in snow. She had a strong dislike for guns, but she knew it's value to her guest, so she shrugged and picked it up.

When she got home, he was sitting up on the pallet, groggy, and fumbling with the bandage about his head. When he saw her, his eyes went wide. "What deviltry is this?" His speech was thick and slurred.

"Oh, shush. You would be dead and buried under three feet of snow if it wasn't for me."

He tried to stand, and she watched him with a bemused smile before she walked over and pushed him down with a gentle touch. "At least stay for dinner." He realized he was naked and pulled the blanket up to his chin. She bustled about before the hearth, making a soup, laced heavily with herbs. She cooked it over the fire as he looked at her from the pallet.

"You have stripped me naked."

Ignorance peeved her, but when people chose ignorance in the face of proof, it made her downright hostile. "I tried to et ya, but you was too tough. This will soften you up."

He pulled the covers up and scuttled back away from her. Then he began praying. She looked into the fire and shook her head while she stirred the pot.

"How did I get here, witch?"

"You should show some thanks, I carried you back here in the storm." She waved back over her shoulder towards the door. "Just now, I got your long gun." She turned to look at him and it was only then he realized she was not an old crone, but a beautiful, young woman.

"You damn fool, you shot at a deer and damn near kilt yerself." She turned back to the fire, decided the soup was done enough, and brought him over a bowl. At first, he waved it off, but her patience was gone. She sat on him, pinning his arms, and pinched his nose. He tried to wrestle free, but his strength was fading fast, so she spooned it into him. As soon as she was done, he passed out. She smiled. "Don't call me a witch again."

The next day, he was able to get out of bed, get dressed, and walk a little, although he had no balance and quickly tired. Wherever she went, he kept to the other side of the room. His speech was better, although it was hard to tell, he was so taciturn and she could only hear him praying under his breath. Charis tried to ignore him, but eventually she faced him, hands on her hips. "You are a damn poor guest. Spend all day ignoring me and talking to somebody ain't even here."

"You said you would eat me."

She looked at him and clucked. "Look around, do you see any bones, or hams? Any leather? I don't eat meat, let alone filthy, stringy pilgrims. Now," she pointed to a chair, "sit."

He looked like he would argue but eventually scuttled around the chair and sat. She checked the wound, although at first he fought her off. He could follow her finger and the pupils were the same size. "You ain't lernt nothing, but it looks like you might live." She turned back to her tasks and heard him praying fervently.

The temperature outside crept up towards freezing and the snow settled. By the fourth day, he was able to stay awake, although he acted distrustful and made the sign of the cross whenever she came by. She began to bore of him and often wondered aloud why she even bothered to save him. When he fashioned a cross out of two sticks and a strip of cloth and stuck it in a crack over his bed, this was too much. She used the last of her valerian root to put him to sleep, then changed his bandage and cleaned his wound. After that she deftly plucked the cross from its perch and tossed it into the fire.

On the fifth day, he was up and about, but sullen. "Where is my crucifix?"

"We don't worship torture here. Besides, that was good firewood. You want to make pagan symbols, you best collect your own wood."

"Blasphemy!"

She went through the wood, and picking one with a Y at the top, thrust it at him. At first, he put his hands up and balked. "It's a crutch, not a cross." She smiled as if she'd made a joke, but still held it out.

Tenuously, Ebidiah reached out and took it. She went over and got his gun. "You don't seem to like being here, so I think it's time you left." She held the door open for him. He gathered up his things and made for the door. When he got there, she put her hand on his chest, and leaned in so close she could smell his breath. "All that praying to your god, and you never once thanked me, who hauled you back in a blizzard and drilled a hole in your head to let the devil out."

He looked at her, his eyes growing wide.

"Boo!" she said. And with that she stepped into the house and shut the door.

It was a week later that she heard them coming on a cold afternoon. Clouds were lowering in preparation for another storm. She opened her door and could see the torch light reflected on the snow as they came. Sometimes the villagers would seek her out, especially the women, for cures. Maybe a family with a sick child, or a farmer with his last cow, but never this many people and never in winter. She wrapped her shawl about her and waited. In ones or twos fear could often conquer ignorance, for a while. But in a mob, fear just fanned the witlessness.

In moments, they were upon her, the Minister of Ignorance, Father Bennett, in the lead. The crowd stopped when the torch light illuminated her, but he continued on, close enough for her to feel the spittle when he hissed, "Witch!"

"I drag a man in from the snow, heal him, give him shelter and succor, and I am a witch?"

"You drilled a hole in his head! You let the devil into him! He died raving and in fever! Is that your cure!"

Her eyes went wide. "Did you not tend the wound?"

"I ripped your foul bandages off, and re-baptized him in holy water, but to no avail. Do you deny your crime?"

Her hand went to her mouth, and her reply was barely heard. "Did you boil it?"

"Boil holy water? A question only a witch would ask!" The snow started to fall in fat flakes, settling on their rough-woven cloaks.

She looked at the crowd and pointed to a man in the front. "Was I a witch when I cured your child last fall, Peter?" She swiveled to point at another. "Who set your son's leg? Who brought milk to your cows?" She pointed to another. "Who helped your good wife conceive?"

"You admit it," spat the priest. Only a devil could do such things."

She looked at him. "And you, who put the devil into your own daughter: who took it out?"

At that, he cried an inaudible scream and reached for her throat, but she adroitly stepped backwards, closed the door, and shot the bolt.

She heard him pounding on the door. The snow on the thatch roof would keep the torches from catching, but she knew they would eventually make a fire that would burn her out. She threw open the rear window, cast a desperate glance around the room, grabbed a satchel and climbed out. She ran straight away from the mob, but in the deep snow it was hard going. She knew that when they found her trail, they would easily run her down, so she climbed to the top of the bowl that protected the house from the wind and circled around. By the time she got even with the cabin front, they had piled wood against the door and started a blaze that was already attacking the walls.

Oh, to be a witch and throw curses upon her enemies.

Instead, she saved her energy and dropped down to the path they had beaten to her door. By the time they figured that out she was not in the cabin and tracked her, the snow would be covering her tracks and they would not be able to follow in the dark. She ran along the beaten path. She fell and sprawled in the blackness, and got up and ran. Over and over, stepping off the path, finding it again, until she found herself at the edge of town.

Faster than she thought possible, she saw the torches behind her. She ran through the village, searching for a place to hide. Finally, the mob drove her to Water Street, the last thing between her and the tide. She went from door-to-door on the slick, muddy street, banging on each and imploring them for mercy. A few candles were lit, but none offered comfort. She could see the torchlight coming down the street, slowed only by the fact that as the mob went door-to-door, people were opening and professing their innocence in harboring the witch. Inflamed with murder-lust, the mob split up to search the houses the faster and continued on, leaving pandemonium in their wake this Christmas Eve.

The last house had a fine brass knocker, shaped like a whale's tail. She was beyond hope as she raised and dropped it, looking at the blackness to her right that was the line of the river. Like hunting a fox, they were pinning her against this barrier. The end was nigh, and she was almost out of fight. She turned from the river and looked at the last bend in the street, the torches must've halted momentarily as they terrorized some poor family. She put her forehead against the glossy burgundy door. *Just a moment to rest,* she thought, and she would make her final push.

When the door opened, she almost fell into the house. A tall, lean man with a neat red beard caught her by the biceps. "Mary!" he called over his shoulder. "Cider, quickly."

He put an arm around Charis, and guided her into the parlor, where a fire warmed the hearth and two wide-eyed children looked at her. He gently put her into a winged-back chair and took the mug his wife proffered. Charis took a sip and shuddered, only then aware of how cold and tired she was. She looked from the children into the eyes of this kind stranger, and realized what a monumental error this was, bringing her horror to this family. She struggled to get up. "I'm sorry, I'm so sorry, I must go."

He laughed. "You just got here."

"You don't understand, there is a mob, they will kill me."

His eyes rolled up dragging his entire head with it until he was looking at the ceiling. "Those damn fools."

"Christian, language. You are in front of children."

"You are the witch?"

Charis nodded, then realized it was a confession. "Not a witch, they called me a witch for healing a man – a man the priest killed."

Christian looked at her. Then shook his head. "Ignorance wrapped in power is the most dangerous brew." He snapped his fingers. "Children, do you believe in witches?"

The children, a boy and a girl, looked back and forth from Christian to Charis. "No sir," said the boy, who looked to be about twelve. The girl looked at her older brother before looking back at Christian and nodding affirmatively.

"So, if somebody asks if you've seen a witch it would be the truth to say 'no.' And we always tell the truth, don't we?"

"Yes sir!" they both answered in unison.

"I think," he said, nodding to the mantle, "that it's time for stockings." The children leapt into action.

Charis tore her gaze from them and looked at Christian. "Why are you doing this?"

"It's the Christian thing to do," he said, and laughed at his own joke.

"Those men claim to be Christians, why would you not give me to them in trade for your soul?"

"I would not trade in any coin they have to offer."

She began to shake, and Mary gently put a blanket on her shoulders. The voices of the mob were clear through the tiny panes of bullseye glass. "What shall we do?"

In answer, Christian spoke to the squealing children who seemed to have forgotten Charis. "Please, take them into the dining room." He bent over and shooed them out with outturned palms like a milkmaid after ducks. He walked over to the hearth, and doing something complex with his fingers under the mantle, opened a cabinet door hidden in the wainscoting. "You, here."

Charis stood up, and walked over to him. "They will burn you out."

"They may try. But, if they burn you and I stand by, I burn anyway."

"But your family."

"My family is my armor. We will stand."

She put one small hand on his chest. "For this boon, I will repay you, many times over."

"Charity and Justice are their own rewards."

"Your god pays in intangibles. I prefer more substantial trade."

"Am I now making a deal with the devil to prove I am a Christian?"

"If I were such a mythical beast, I might prefer to be an angel."

"Then I am paid already."

"Take my bargain. I will protect you. Refuse it, and I will walk into the street."

Christian turned to look at Mary. She shrugged, but was clearly nervous, twisting her apron strings in her fingers. "Stop babbling and put her in the cupboard, whatever deal it may take."

"I ask these simple things: every Christmas Eve set out a bowl of porridge to sustain me. In it put a drop of blood, to prove your enduring faith. A coin of gold to acknowledge our bargain, and a glass of your finest wine to renew it."

"And for this?"

"For this, all of your ships will return from sea. Your business will prosper. No sons will ever die at war. All of your babies will live long lives. And this will be true for their sons and daughters as long as this family shall own this house and celebrate Christmas here."

At that moment, there was a great pounding on the door, and they did not use the fine brass knocker, but a cudgel or fist.

"Done," said the Captain, grabbing her by the shoulder

and all but throwing her into the cubby. She turned in the cramped space, a little L-shaped cupboard that went behind the chimney, it's sloping ceiling created by the stairs and their landing as they turned halfway up.

"Do not forget, Captain." They locked eyes and he felt a shock to the soles of his feet. "If you do these simple things, I will be your liege, and guard your house. If you fail, it will break my bond, and I will seek a vessel for freedom."

"I will not forget: porridge, blood, gold, and wine. We will talk on the morrow." The racket at the door sounded as if they would break it down. The cupboard door slammed shut, and even knowing it was there, Christian could not see any evidence of it from the outside.

The Captain turned and said to Mary, "Mind the children. It's Christmas Eve and we are a family celebrating." She went into the dining room on the other side of the hall, and he opened the door.

"What blasphemy is this?" He looked at the rag-tag mob, somewhat dispirited by the snow, the late hour, and the failed search.

"I would ask the same," spat the priest. "She is nowhere else, she must be here."

"Whom do you seek?" Again he cast his gaze to the crowd. "If this is some passion play, w e have no manger here." Laughs broke out.

"Enough insolence. Your antagonism to our Lord God is well known. Let us in to search for the witch." He tried to push past Christian, but the man stopped him with a hand to his chest.

"Do not mistake my shunning of your poison for a lack of faith, *priest*. It will take more than mania to get past me."

The group began to mutter. Some pushed forward, but others seemed to lose their appetite for the night's pastime.

"Yield, or pay the consequences." He raised his torch and shook it, sparks showering the Captain.

Christian looked up the street. His neighbors had drifted to the edge of the confrontation.

"If my house burns, all of the houses burn. Would you pay that price to assuage this madman? You," he punctuated his address with a meaty finger to the priest's chest, "are not welcome in my house on this holy night, or on any night hereafter." He leaned in so that only the priest could hear him. "And if you don't stop tending to your daughter how you tend to your flock, I will burn *your* house out."

With a howl of rage, the priest drew back his torch and threw it into the house. It landed on the dry wood of the stairs. When Christian turned to grab it, the priest pushed past him, and his newly galvanized followers followed. Mary and the children huddled in one corner of the dining room. Christian lost his battle with the mob. The priest bounded past Christian and up the stairs. The rest poured into the house and searched it from top to bottom. When the priest came down the stairs, Christian stood there with the quenched torch and his dignity.

As they passed, the priest's eyes glowed with fanaticism. "We will find her, and when we do, your part will be exposed."

Christian reared to his full height and smote the priest, breaking his nose and knocking him out. Then, grabbing him by the back of his cloak, dragged him into the street. "I call this man murderer. It was he who killed the good man Ebidiah with his backwoods doctoring. I sentence him to banishment, from his parish, his house, his village, and his family. Whosoever harbors him, faces me. Who would gainsay me this?" Murmurs went through the crowd and some began to protest, but Christian merely lifted the inert clergyman by one hand, blood streaming down his face onto his cloak. He shook him like a dog shakes a rat and the priest started to come to. "To the birth of Christ and the death of tyranny," he shouted. There were a few hear -hear s from the crowd. Tossing the priest into the mud, Christian said, "Explain his punishment to him," and turned to go inside.

At that moment, he looked up, and the crowd turned. The street was on fire, and it leapt from house to house as spritely as old St. Nick. People screamed in shock. The idiots, someone in the other group must've gotten carried away. The crowd dispersed, each to their own, to see what could be saved. Christian assessed the situation and sprinted inside.

Mary held the kids, huddled against her skirts in the corner. He went over to them, crouched down and swept them all up in a hug while he shushed them and quieted their tears. "Get them dressed." Bells began to ring, and a wagon clattered by up front. "The fire brigade will be pumping water from the river and they'll need my help if anything is to be saved. I'll get Claris out of the cupboard, put a few things in a sack, and head to the old mill pond. I will find you there."

Mary nodded, sweeping the kids up too quickly for protest .Christian went into the parlor and unlatched the cupboard. When Charis did not come out, he lit a tallow and, getting on his hands and knees, crawled in looking for her. The dust wasn't even disturbed. As he was backing out, Mary came into the room. "Where is our guest?"

He stood up and brushed the dust from his trousers. "Gone. Like she was never here."

When he was done Tim, who had reached the Age of Doubt, asked, "Did that really happen, Dad?"

"Well, there was a time when people were very ignorant and superstitious, so I believe it really did happen. My dad believed it, I believed him, he believed his dad, and so forth."

"Yeah, but the whole disappearing thing?" said Tim.

"Lots of ways to explain that, I'm sure."

"Oh," said Sarah, "the lady in the cupboard didn't disappear, I talk to her all of the time."

Brin stood bolt upright. "What?"

"The Lady who lives behind the fireplace. Sometimes she comes out and talks to me." Sarah stood up, made a little curtsey, and did what Thayer thought was the first unsteady steps of an Irish reel. "She's teaching me to dance." Brin and Thayer exchanged a glance.

Brin stood up and clapped her hands. "That's enough for tonight, run up and get ready for bed." The kids did the requisite protesting but eventually took off. Brin's eyes twinkled like icicles. "That is the last time you tell that story. Sarah is going to need therapy."

"For having an imaginary friend that doesn't live in a video game?"

"I'm done having this conversation. She's not your daughter, and she's not healthy. What do you think it's like for her to hear that story? It makes Tim special and she's... she's nothing. Next year, we are having Christmas in the city. Mind the fire and turn off the lights when you come up."

Thayer twirled the wine stem and stared into the fire. That cut hurt, as much and more so than Brin intended, he was sure. When Sarah was born, they said she'd never walk, but every time they came here, she got a little better. A dance! What more did Brin need to believe? Didn't that prove that Sarah was as much a part of this as Tim? Ah, hell, at least that fight wasn't going to happen for another year. He then downed his brandy in a slug, put the offerings on a small table to the left of the fire that was there just for the purpose, pouring the last of the excellent Burgundy into a child-size wine glass. When he locked up, fat flakes were drifting down in the street lights outside. A white Christmas was like a fresh sheet of paper to write the new year upon. He and Brin would get through this, he thought, locking up and going to bed.

His phone blared him awake after midnight, he looked quickly at the caller ID as he picked up. "Karl, what the hell? It's Christmas Eve – he saw the clock – morning."

"Thayer, we lost a ship in the North Atlantic. It was covered in ice and when a rogue wave hit it, it went over. It's just…gone. We got one chaotic mayday and nothing. No radar, nothing."

When Thayer sat bolt upright it wasn't the icy draft that chilled him. "Karl, that can't be. We haven't lost a ship in our entire history."

"Well, we lost one now."

Thayer rested his forehead in his hand. His brain could not parse this information. His thoughts raced over the evening. What could've gone wrong? What did he forget? Brin was awake, watching him. "Thayer, what's wrong."

He looked at her, forgetting he was on the line with Karl. "We lost a ship. We've never lost a ship. Every year, I tell the story, I put out the tribute…"

The smoke detector began shrieking. He spared one moment to look at Brin and shook his head before he leapt out of bed. Timmy's room was first on the left and he burst through the door, ripping the covers off the bed in the same motion. When he bent to pick his son up, he weighed almost nothing in his arms. Looking down in the hallway light, he could see the boy's face. It had no eyes, and when his mouth dropped open, liquid gold poured out. It just poured and poured a pure liquid metallic vomit and where it hit Thayer's chest it burned him like charred meat. He shrieked and held the body away from him, but didn't drop it. Other than the gold, the body was just a desiccated shell of skin, as if Tim died centuries ago. The gold finally stopped, and Christian instinctively pulled Tim back to hold him. To Thayer's horror, when he clutched the body to his chest, it broke into pieces that slid out of the pajamas and fell on the bed in dusty fragments. Thayer was frantically trying to pick them up while the alarm shrieked, and he became dimly aware of smoke filling the room.

Brin ran by. "Sarah's gone!"

Thayer tore himself away from his futile efforts and turned to follow, stopping at the door to confirm what he already knew but couldn't believe. His son. His son was gone. The first child lost in how long?

Brenda was downstairs, trying to get into the living room but it appeared to be the center of the blaze. Thayer stopped at the base of the stairs and grabbed her, barely able to keep her from throwing herself into the flames. Through them he could see, the cupboard door was open, and Sarah's crutches lay there, but otherwise the room was empty. The heat was so intense it burned off his eyelashes and the hair off his unclad upper body, creating a fine layer of ash.

When he finally pried Brin off the door frame, he dragged her through the door into the yard. Then he carried her out into the street where they stood together arms wrapped around each other. Thayer kept repeating "I don't understand. I don't understand, the tribute…"

Brin looked up at him. "That silly thing! I tossed that out when I got up to pee."

Thayer pushed her at arms' length and held her by the shoulders. "You what?"

"I just thought it was my job," she sobbed. "Like my dad, eating Santa's cookies. Somebody had to keep up the pretense…"

Thayer shook her. "What have you done?"

"I told you I was done with it. I threw it out. It's idolatry, and it's affecting Sarah."

"But Sarah was getting better," he mumbled too quietly for her to hear.

People were out on the street now, and he could hear sirens. Thayer let go of Brin and collapsed to his knees in the new-fallen snow, and there, heading toward the river, were a set of tiny footprints almost full of snow.

9

THE DUCK MAN

I. CLAYTON REYNOLDS

*T*he night was calm and peaceful before the strange animal call broke it. Long trails of white and amber light reflected across the polished glass surface of the lake at the bottom of the hill. Lucia and I had walked back to her sister's place, where I left my pickup truck parked. We had gone down the street to a pre-Christmas party from there after handing the kids off to her sister. Lucia held close to me. I don't know if it was to keep warm, or because we had a fun night and she wanted to be close. I didn't really care. Having her hold on to me felt good, and I wasn't going to spoil it with questions.

The kids were still sleeping when we placed them in their seats, having carried them out. Lucia stopped me before I could climb in the driver's seat.

"You have had a few too many tonight, mister. Hand me those keys," she said. I smiled and handed them over.

I was rounding the bumper to the passenger fender when

I heard a noise. I stopped. I looked at Lucia. "Did you hear that?"

Lucia stood still with her mouth open. A slow stream of fog escaped her mouth as she stared. I whipped my head in the direction of her stare, and I saw nothing. I heard the noise again.

It sounded like a duck, but not a short quack. It was long as if the duck were in pain or frightened out of its mind. It had a staccato quality to it that was almost mechanical. A ratcheting sound. I knew right away what was happening.

"Come on out, guys," I said. I began walking toward the row of hedges on the opposite corner. Dusty and Bill were messing with me, trying to scare me. I wasn't *that* drunk.

I was about halfway to the intersection when Lucia broke her silence. In a voice not much above a whisper she said, "Don't. Stay here."

The noise came again. This time I felt as much as heard it. My gut tightened and a bout of nausea hit me. I had to hold back vomit. Maybe I was *that* drunk.

I turned to look at Lucia. She stood stiff next to the truck, her eyes still focused on the intersection. I looked again and still saw nothing.

"Come on, guys. Quit being stupid."

I stepped back toward the curb when I heard the roar of a vehicle coming from over the hill. As the truck crested the hill, it came to a quick stop at the stop sign. At that moment, a Jeep came from the south, lighting up the intersection. The Jeep had the right of way and no stop sign, but it screeched to a stop at the intersection. I recognized the Jeep as Derek's. We had just come from Derek's house, his party.

The duck noise came again, louder and higher. Again I felt the urge to puke. The truck banged into reverse and spun its tires as it backed from the intersection and then took off forward down an alley. It was my friend Dusty's truck.

I could hear the engine winding up as if he was running some kind of a race. Derek turned toward his house and sped away.

I went to the passenger door of my truck and got in. Lucia followed my cue and got behind the wheel.

"Go down there to Derek's," I said.

"What was that?" she said.

"I don't know. Were they racing somewhere?"

"No, I mean that thing."

I looked at her. "You mean the sound? I don't know. It was weird--"

"No," she said, "I mean the big white thing. With the blanket over it."

"I guess I didn't see it."

She took a deep breath and started the truck. Cold air blasted from the vents at my feet.

"What do you mean, you didn't see it?" she said.

"I don't know what you're talking about. I saw the guys stop at the intersection fast, then take off again."

She threw the truck in drive and took off.

We arrived at Derek's just as Dusty pulled up. I met up with them in the driveway.

"What the hell was that?" Derek said. Dusty shook his head with raised eyebrows.

"What were y'all doing?" I said.

Dusty said, "I was chasing that thing. I had it on the floor and it was outrunning me. What the hell?"

"What thing?" I asked. Both Derek and Dusty looked shaken.

Derek said, "We saw something. I don't know what. Up there at the top of the hill. I almost hit it with my pickup."

"Yeah, I was right there when you slammed on your brakes."

"You saw it then," Derek said.

"I didn't see anything. I just heard a noise."

"It looked like a guy with a white blanket over his head," Dusty said, "except it was about eight feet tall. Tall as my pickup cab...and faster."

I turned to look at Lucia, who was standing in the dry, yellow grass. She nodded. Her eyes were wide and I could see her hands shaking.

"I'm cold," Derek said. "I'm going inside. I'll see y'all later."

"Yeah I need to get the kids home." I looked toward the truck and I could see movement in the back seat. "I'll see y'all sometime this week. I want to hear more about this."

"Hell, you done heard about all I know," said Dusty. "It was tall, fast and white."

It was a week before I saw either of them, and Lucia and I had not spoken about it again. I happened upon both of them at Hazel's Boat House, a restaurant on the lake front. Derek was having catfish with his wife. Dusty was at the bar with a bottle of beer and a skinny blonde that I didn't know.

"So, tell me what you saw the other night?" I said to Derek, whose booth was next to our table.

"When?"

"After the party. On Juniper Street."

"What? I went to the store after the party and got some burritos and a Coke. That's about it."

"I mean the tall thing with the blanket over his head. You got to the intersection of Juniper and Lake, and you skidded to stop. You said you almost hit him, the guy or whatever it was."

Derek lowered his brow and showed me a puzzled expression. He half smiled and said, "I don't know what you're talking about."

"Lucia, will you back me up here? Tell him what I'm talking about."

"I don't know what you're talking about. The waitress has been here twice. Are you going to order?"

"Dusty," I called to the bar. I called a second time before I got his attention. He walked over with the blonde in tow. She stood behind him and did not speak. Dusty did not introduce her.

"Dusty, remember last week after the party when you saw what looked like a tall guy covered in a blanket and you chased him down the alley in your truck? Tell me what you saw exactly."

Dusty took a long pull from his long-neck beer bottle, then dropped his face and looked at the floor, removing his cap enough to scratch his head. He started shaking his head as he lifted it. "What are you talking about?" he said.

"After the party. I saw both of you stop at the intersection of Juniper and Lake. Lucia drove me down to Derek's and you both told me you saw an eight foot tall guy with a blanket over his head." I turned to Lucia. "You said the same thing."

"I remember you pulling up with your kids in the truck right when I was leaving. I said 'see you tomorrow,' and you left. I didn't see no guy with a blanket on his head," Dusty said.

I could see that Dusty was holding back a laugh. Maybe he thought I was crazy. More likely, I was right all along. There was someone in the bushes playing a prank. After all, I never saw anything. I just heard the weird duck sound. And, Lucia must have been in on it.

I spent the rest of dinner watching for interaction between Dusty, Derek, and Lucia. Looking for a wink, a nod, or a knowing look. But, there was nothing. They all went about their business and Lucia only said, "Goodbye, Dustin," as we left.

Later that night, actually early Sunday morning, I was driving the one county road that cut through the Kilderry, a part of the county that was once a thriving oil pool, but was now a wasteland. Only a few people lived out there. Mostly it was overgrown with impassible underbrush strung around post oaks. I was returning from the Harper place in the service truck. They called around midnight saying their furnace was out. It was supposed to be well below freezing overnight. Not a good night to be without a furnace.

Like many folks who lived out past the Kilderry, the Harpers didn't have much. They couldn't afford things like routine maintenance on their home, so they ended up out of luck on the first really cold night. I couldn't even charge them extra for an after-hours call. They couldn't pay it if I did. I'd charge them for the new igniter, but that was it. Price of doing business. Merry Christmas to them and happy holidays to me.

I was still a mile or so from the paved Farm to Market road when something large blew across the road in front of me like a speeding ball of smoke. I mashed the brakes and my truck came to rest at a 30 degree angle to the road. I looked and saw a path of damage where branches were broken and weeds were smashed flat. The barbed wire fence was laid over, it's metal posts bent almost parallel to the ground. That was as far as I could see with the truck's headlights.

I grabbed the Maglite from behind the seat and clicked the button. I rested the black metal end on my shoulder as I guided the beam with my hand. The path of destruction continued past the fence.

I caught the reflection of an animal's eyes. Two together. A bobcat or a coyote, I thought…until it stood.

A large, pale mass rose from the weeds and stood at a height taller than any human. A coat of flowing hair like that of an Afghan hound draped its body. It turned its head away and I lost sight of it for a moment and then I saw its eyes turn back, this time closer to the road.

It let loose its whining howl, this time much more furious than what I had heard in town. The same nausea came over me as before and in waves, the figure seemed to disappear from view.

I dropped the light in the seat without bothering to shut it off and pressed the accelerator to the floor. I began to vomit down the front of my shirt, but I was too afraid to stop.

I was giving the old work truck all it had and doing my best to keep it on the road. I glanced in the side mirror and saw that the monster was visible in my tail lights. It was keeping pace with me.

I felt my balls crawl up inside me and my heart try to crawl out of me. I was coming upon the intersection with the highway and knew I would have to slow down to make the turn. I checked the mirror again. The beast was gone. I checked all three mirrors and even tapped the brakes to offer more illumination behind. It was no longer behind me.

"I saw it," I told Lucia when I got home. She was asleep, but I was too wound up to let her stay that way. "I saw the duck man. It was tall and hairy. It had long white hair that hung off of it like a blanket. Like it was wearing a blanket. Just like you said. It made that sound, the howling/quacking sound. I saw it."

Lucia had her head raised and her hand was shading her

eyes. She looked at me through slits of eyelids. "What time is it?" she said.

"Did you hear me? I saw it."

"Yeah. You saw your duck man. Good for you. Good night." She dropped her head back onto the pillow and rolled the blanket over her. I don't know what I expected, but it was a disappointing reaction. I went to the kids' rooms and checked on them and then went to bed.

My mind was racing. I had trouble falling asleep. I got up, had some snacks, and wrapped some gifts. Twice, I checked the locks on the house. Halfway through the second check, I began to feel foolish, not only for thinking a monster might come to my house, but also for thinking it would use the doors properly. It was miles away. I returned to bed.

I tried to talk about it. Derek, Dusty, and Lucia all continued to deny seeing the thing. I was forced to examine my own sanity. But I knew what I saw and what I heard.

What was I going to do? I wasn't going to go hunting for it. I had no witnesses. All I had was a good campfire story. The outcome could have been worse.

As the week went on, the duck man traveled further toward the back of my mind. Life went on and the reality of the experience waned.

One week before Christmas, it turned warm outside. The weather around here, who can figure it out? Lucia and I slept in the cool night with the window opened a crack. The fresh air was nice, as were the smells of the night. The organic sweetness of the fallen leaves and winter grass was comforting.

In the distance I could hear dogs barking, and even further away, a train's whistle. I heard a car drive down the street. And somewhere, a few blocks away maybe, I heard a sound like the scream of a rabid duck.

I jerked upright in bed and Lucia did the same. I looked at her and could see the wonder on her face. She was hearing it.

"What is that?" she said to me as she felt around the night stand for her glasses. Once she had them, she reached for the lamp.

"Don't," I said. "Leave the light off. I want to look out the window."

"What is it, David?"

"It's the sound I've been telling you about. The duck sound. It's out there."

"Oh, God." Lucia got up and tried to look out the window over my shoulder.

The street was as peaceful as ever. Colored lights decorated trees and white lights hung from eaves. Everyone was asleep in their beds, peaceful in their ignorance of a monster in the neighborhood.

I heard the sound again, and I turned to Lucia. She was gone. I left the room and went into the hallway. The light was on in the bathroom and the door was closed. I paced the hallway, waiting. I looked into the kids' rooms. They both seemed fine. Aaron was sprawled out on top the covers like he had fallen from a tall building. Daniela was rolled up in her blanket, flanked on either side by plush stuffed animals.

I heard the door click and Lucia came out into the hall and turned toward our bedroom. I followed.

She turned to me and raised an eyebrow. "What are you doing up?"

"I'm nervous. I don't know what it is. It's scary."

"What is?"

"The duck man."

"Ay ay ay, honey. Are you going on about that again? I'm getting worried about you. Scary stories are one thing, but when you are up fretting in the night... Let's go to bed."

I stood with my jaw hanging down to my chest. What the hell was happening? We had both heard the sound not ten minutes earlier.

"What do you think that sound was?"

"I told you, I didn't hear a sound. I just saw you yelling across the street."

"No, Lucia. I mean just a few minutes ago. The sound that woke us up. The duck man sound from outside."

She said nothing. She just stared. The look on her face said it all. It was a look of pity. She felt bad for me. She thought I was cracking up. I think if I looked in a mirror, the man staring back at me would think the same thing.

It happened again the next night. It was closer this time. It was louder. Lucia sprung out of bed before I did. She was hyperventilating and barely got out, "What the hell is that?"

I shot to the window and scanned the street. The moon was high and the neighborhood was well lit. I saw nothing. I turned around and Lucia stood, breathing hard, and holding a hand to her chest.

"You heard it?"

She nodded.

"What did it sound like?"

"Like a long, yelling quack. Just like you said."

I switched on the lamp and stretched across the bed. I grabbed the paperback book from my nightstand and folded over the back cover. I took a pen from the drawer. I stood and handed them both to Lucia.

"Write down that you heard it."

"What?"

"Write it down, so you can remember."

"Jesus, David. I'll remember."

"You did not remember last time. Write it down."

She began to write with her shaking hands. When I was satisfied that she had written enough, I held out my hand and she gave me the book. I put it on the bed and turned off the lamp. I returned to the window.

I stayed back a couple of steps in the darkness of the room. I did not want it to see me. Then I remembered when I shined the Maglite on its face. I remember the reflection. Tapetum lucidum. It meant the beast had night vision like other nocturnal animals. It could likely see me just fine. Maybe not. How dark was dark enough?

I went through the house, shutting down anything that made light. The clock on the microwave oven, the night lights in the kids' rooms. Even that damned little red LED on the TV that was to alert me that it was turned off…as if I could not figure that out on my own.

When I got back, Lucia was in bed, asleep. She had forgotten by now, I guessed. I wondered if writing it down might have left a mark on her memory. I decided not to wake her. At least I had her own handwriting to show her.

I closed the window and locked it. I walked around the bed. When I sat on my side, I picked up the paperback from the mattress and put it in the nightstand drawer. Somehow, I managed to fall asleep.

Lucia did not remember a thing. I could not understand. How does one forget something like that? I was proud of myself for thinking to have her write it down. I could confirm not only to her that she heard the thing, but it was also insurance against my own doubt. It is a short trip to self-doubt when I know something happened and everyone else knows it didn't.

I retrieved the book from the drawer and headed out of the room toward the kitchen. As I walked, I flipped open the back cover and stopped dead in my tracks. Instead of an unprinted page with my wife's shaky handwriting, there was a paragraph with the title, "About the Author."

It was my turn to hyperventilate. I had gone mad, sure as shit. Completely fucking cuckoo. Off the deep end. The blank page on which I thought I had her write did not even exist. I flipped it over to look at the cover. It was the correct book. Same gold lettering. Same painting of a desert highway.

I returned to the bedroom and sat on the bed. I tried my best to remember everything. Could it have been a dream? It was too vivid. Everything in the house was unplugged just like I remembered leaving it. The book was where I remembered putting it. The window was closed and locked.

I looked around the room. I remembered all of it. I noticed at the baseboard under the window and next to Lucia's nightstand something that looked like a large white bean. I stooped over and reached for it.

It seemed to be a large spit wad, still slightly wet. I remembered making these in school by chewing up notebook paper. The notebook paper with its lines would produce a ball of mush with a blue-white color. This was more yellowed. More the color of the pages of the paperback book in my hand.

I began to take the wad of pulp apart. It mostly disintegrated in my hands. I did eventually see tiny bits with the blue lines of ink made by a shaky hand. There wasn't enough of it to prove what it was to anyone else, but I knew.

I opened the back cover of the book and I could see where the page had been torn from the binding. Lucia had taken this a bit too far.

I strode into the kitchen and showed her what I found. I asked her how she could do it, how she could make me think I was losing my mind. She kept up the charade. She denied knowing anything at all. I dressed and went to work.

By the end of the day, it got cold again. The weather lady hinted that there could be snow for Christmas. I went to Hazel's instead of home. I sat at the bar, knocking back more mugs of beer than I should. Like clockwork, Dusty came in just after six, stood at the end of the bar, and ordered a long-neck. I gave him a nod.

I was more certain than ever that all of this was an elaborate prank. Dusty, who was not someone who would ever be called a mastermind, gave no indication that he knew about anything. He didn't crack a smile. He didn't act overly concerned or feign interest. If he was in on some kind of prank, he needed to get to Hollywood, because he was giving the performance of a lifetime.

I didn't know what to think. I was angry when I talked to Lucia, but in retrospect she was no less convincing than Dusty. The more I thought about it, the more impossible it seemed that what I saw on the county road that night was a hoax. No one could have known I would be there at that time. I did not mistake some other animal for an eight foot tall beast. And the eyes. Would any of my friends have gone to the trouble to fake that detail?

I drove home, though I probably should have called Lucia for a ride. I just wasn't sure she would come get me. When I walked inside, everyone was sitting together on the couch watching TV with a bowl of popcorn. I went into the kitchen and sat at the table. A cold plate of food sat there, covered in plastic wrap. I buried my face in the palms of my hands.

Lucia entered the kitchen and sat down. She touched my arm with her hand and asked , "Are you okay?"

My chest hitched and a snort escaped my nose. I was unsure at first if it was a sob or a laugh. It was both. I laughed as the tears rolled down my cheeks.

"I'm so sorry," I said. "I'm so, so sorry."

She patted my arm and gave a half-hearted smile. "We'll survive, dear. Things just got carried away."

"Yeah," I said. The laughter was gone from my sobs.

"I think you should take some time off," Lucia said. "We could go away for a few days after Christmas is done. Stay someplace nice. We could take the kids to the museums or something. Or, we could just relax and hang out in a hotel room and order pizza. What do ya say?"

"I *have* been promising to take Daniela to the Children's Museum for several months. Let's do it. We'll stay a few nights at a hotel on the river. Something with a view. I'll tell the guys at work first thing in the morning."

"Daniela was pretty worried about you. You should go talk to her."

"I suppose I should. Is she in the living room?"

"No. I sent the kids to bed before I came in here."

I nodded and stood. I walked to Daniela's room.

Daniela stood on her bed, staring out the window. Her light was off and she did not seem to notice me enter the room. I sat on the end of the bed, not too close because I did not want to make her stumble.

"Hey girly, I wanted to talk to you and see how you're doing," I said.

She continued staring out the window.

"Are you not talking to me?" I said. She gave no reaction. I continued, "Look, I'm sorry. Mom and I had a fight, and I got too upset. I shouldn't have left like that. I'm sorry I scared you and upset you. From now on I'm going to work to be a little more patient. Okay? Daniela?"

The girl didn't move a muscle. She just stared out the

window with her arms at her side and her head cocked. She held a teddy bear by a leg in her left hand. Her bare feet planted in the soft mattress of her bed.

"Dani? Daniela?" I called.

When she still did not react, I stood and walked toward the window. When I got close enough, I looked at Daniela's face. Her expression was blank. I gazed out the window to see what she might be watching.

The night was clear and moonlight illuminated the back-yard and alleyway. I could see the swing set and the garbage cans, but nothing out of the ordinary. I turned back to Daniela and she was locked on me, grinning.

"Hi, Daddy," she said.

"Hi, Girly. Did you not hear me come in?"

"No. Sorwy, I was watching."

"What were you watching, sweetie?"

"The no-man."

"The no man?"

"No, not the no man, the 'no' man."

"Do you mean, snowman?"

"Yes. He was by the fence looking at me."

I felt my skin tighten and a shiver march through me.

"What did the snowman look like, sweetie?"

"Big and hairy and white like on Woo-doff the wane-deer. The bom-a-bull no-man. I think he wants to take me to meet Santa Claus."

I could barely get my next words out. "The snowman was out there at the fence and was looking at you? How do you know it was looking at you?"

"I waved at him. He waved back."

I didn't want to alarm her, so I did my best to conceal my panic. I pressed my shaking hands against my thighs and cleared my throat.

"Dani," I said, my voice cracking, "w ould you like to sleep in mine and mommy's room tonight? Both of you can in your sleeping bags. It will be like a campout."

"Yes. That's fun, Daddy."

I picked her up and hugged her close. I carried her with me through the house, not wanting her out of my sight. I roused her brother and he took his sleeping bag to the master bedroom. I returned to Daniela's bedroom and got her pink princess sleeping bag from the closet.

Lucia was in the bedroom when we all arrived.

"What is this?" she asked. She made a slow exaggerated gasp faking excitement for our fun little sleepover.

I exited the room with the intention of double checking every lock in the house. Lucia followed me into the hallway.

"What are we doing?" she asked.

I turned and walked toward her, not wanting her to stray too far from the bedroom.

"Daniela told me she saw a snowman standing by the fence looking at her and that it waved back at her when she waved to it. It's the fucking duck man. He's outside somewhere."

"She probably heard you talking about the fool thing, and her imagination went wild."

"I don't think so. I was talking to her and she didn't even hear me. She was staring out the window at something. She was transfixed on it."

"You're acting as though you believe this 'duck man' is real."

"Dammit, it is real. You have heard it. You can't remember. No one can seem to remember but me."

"Yeah, would you quit saying that? You sound like a lunatic, David."

"Would you quit saying that and believe me? Or don't believe me, or whatever. Just stay in there with the kids while I lock the doors. I feel better having them in our room tonight. Is that okay?"

"Well, I can't very well kick them out now. So, okay, they can stay in our room."

"Go back in there, Lucia, please. I don't want them left alone. I don't know what's going on, but I want to be safe. I'm going to go check all the locks."

Lucia sighed and returned to the bedroom. I went through the house watching out the windows and listening as I went. I neither saw nor heard anything. With everything checked out, I returned to the bedroom. I locked the bedroom door.

The kids were already asleep. I expected them to be up chattering all night, so it was a relief. I got in bed with Lucia and put my arms around her.

"Are you okay?" Lucia said to me.

"I don't know," I said. "I just don't know."

I was startled when I woke because I was surprised I had been asleep. I had lain in bed for hours listening for any noise at all and was sure I could not fall asleep. But I must have drifted off at some point. Time had passed and I had been dreaming, about what, I could not remember.

The bedroom door stood open. I sat up in bed to find everyone accounted for. Someone must have gone to the bathroom and left it open.

A glance at the window told me it was still dark out. I decided to have a look around before trying to get some more sleep.

I went down the hallway looking in each bedroom. All looked okay. I mentally made a note to turn up the heat on the thermostat when I got there. I hadn't noticed when I was in the bedroom, but it was chilly in the house.

I went into the living room and then into the kitchen. That is where I stopped.

The back door was standing wide open. I froze for a moment and then backtracked into the living room. I grabbed the poker from the fireplace and stepped into the kitchen, peeking around the door frame before going through.

I made my way to the open back door. Cold air blew in from outside while the night dragged away the heat. I peered around the edge of the doorway checking the outside area for any danger. I saw nothing.

I pulled the screen shut and latched it. I had not locked the screen, but I did now. I grabbed the wooden door and pushed it closed. It caught before it closed. The latch was busted. Both the doorknob bolt and the deadbolt were ripped out of the door from impact. The doorjamb itself was also torn away.

I worked the deadbolt back and pushed the door closed. I

placed a jug of laundry detergent in front of the door to keep it from swinging open.

I again searched the house, turning on every light as I went. Someone (or something) had broken into the house and could still be inside. I checked each room, closet, and nook. I did not find anyone or anything .

It was Christmas Eve, and the shop was closed. I called one of my workers at home and let him know I would be gone for a week. Christmas or no, we were getting out of town. We would take the gifts with us and have Christmas on Christmas morning, but somewhere else.

I got on the computer to find a place to stay and make reservations for our trip. Instead, I found myself looking at cryptozoology sites trying to find some explanation of what the duck man might be. I found plenty of info regarding Bigfoot, Sasquatch, the yeti, and so on, but nothing that fit exactly. After about twenty minutes, I was interrupted by a tremendous crash from outside.

I ran to the front door and threw it open. A blue SUV had crashed into my parked truck and flipped over into the driveway onto the back of Lucia's car.

I ran to the wreckage and found the driver, a teenage boy, hanging from the seatbelt with an airbag over his face.

"Are you okay?" I called to him from down on my knees. The roof was caved to the point that his head was cocked sideways against it.

"I think so," said the boy.

I stuck my head inside and looked him over as best as I could. He had cuts with minor bleeding but nothing life threatening as far as I could see.

Lucia was beside me when I got back out and onto my knees.

"Call the police, Luce," I said. Then to the kid in the pickup, "Just stay where you are. Don't move. Let's let the guys who know what they are doing handle this. I'm afraid that if I try to get you out, I'll make things worse."

"Get me out," said the kid. His voice was quavering and he started to wriggle in the seatbelt.

"No, you have got to stay still."

The kid kept moving. He managed to get his seatbelt loose and he collapsed to the roof of the cab. A dam broke somewhere and torrents of blood rolled from beneath his body.

"Shit," I said, and grabbed his arm and pulled him from the wreck. I rolled him over to find a large gash in his back. Something had cut or stabbed into him, and it was deep.

Lucia was still inside. No one was there. Where were the goddamn neighbors? I ran inside and grabbed the full stack of dish towels from the kitchen drawer.

I wadded one and stuffed it down into the wound. I grabbed more, pressed and held and tried to stop the bleeding, but it kept coming. I grabbed another towel, folded it and pressed with the other hand. No good. I grabbed another.

There were enough towels now that more was not going to do anything. The towels were saturated with blood and it looked like I had done little more than slow the flow.

"You still with me, kid?" I said. There was no answer.

Lucia came out of the house and said an ambulance was on the way. I could already hear its siren in the distance.

"Wake up kid, your ride is on the way."

I looked up to Lucia. "See if you can get him awake."

She nudged him and yelled "hello" into his ears. He gave no response. The yellow-brown winter grass around him had turned a peculiar, deep reddish brown color. Lucia's hands had smudges of bright glossy red on them from where she had put her hand on his back to shake him awake.

Lucia put her hands on the kid's neck to feel for a pulse. She shook her head and grabbed his wrist. She shook her head again.

"I can't feel a pulse," she said.

"What do we do?"

"CPR, I guess."

"If I roll him over, he's going to lose the rest of his blood."

"If you don't," Lucia said, "h e's already dead."

The ambulance was still several blocks away. I considered holding the blood until they arrived, but seconds counted in this situation.

"Can you do CPR?" I asked Lucia.

"Yes, I can."

"Roll him over. I'm going to keep my hands on his back underneath to try to hold in the blood."

Lucia pushed with both hands and I grabbed with one and we rolled the kid over. Lucia started chest compressions and I tried to hold the towels tight in the wound.

She was on the third round of compressions when the ambulance arrived. The paramedics took over. They put a defibrillator on him attempting to shock him back. It was no good. They put him in the ambulance and the EMT's continued to do chest compressions while they whisked him away to the hospital.

As the ambulance pulled away, I saw that the neighbors

were out of their houses and looking on. I grumbled and turned to go inside. A police officer insisted I stay until he filled out some paper or another. He had a lot of questions and the blood was a dry sticky paste on my skin before he finished.

When I was at last free to go in and clean up, I saw the kids standing outside the front door. I had no idea how long they had been there or how much they saw. They might have seen all of it. They might have seen that kid die right there while I tried to stop up his new drain hole. Whether they did or not, they saw me now, and I was covered with drying human blood. I had to be a frightening sight and the look on the kids' faces confirmed that.

"Go back inside," I said. They hurried through the door. When I looked back, Lucia was spraying the red spot on the lawn with the garden hose.

It was too late to go anywhere, and both vehicles were out of commission. Lucia's might have a chance, but my truck was a goner.

I had underestimated the damage to the back door. I went to see what I needed to change the doorknob and it was no use. The doorjamb was damaged beyond what I could repair with a simple hammer and nails. I tacked a piece of wood up to the frame to hold the door closed for the night. The storm door was locked, and the solid door could not be opened from the outside, although a good kick could do away with both doors. It would have to do.

I entered the kitchen and found Daniela standing on a chair, looking out the front window. Gooseflesh rose on my arms.

"Daniela," I said.

She turned to me immediately. The steel came out of my shoulders. I expected her to be entranced as she was the night before.

"Look, Daddy. It's 'no-ing."

I walked over to the chair and took her in my arms. "Let's go see."

I carried her to the front door. I opened it and we stepped out onto the porch. Big flakes of snow were falling. The temperature had dropped over the last few hours and he thought the snow just might accumulate if there was enough.

"It's pretty, isn't it?" I said.

"Yes, pretty 'no," she said.

I smiled at her as she smiled at the snowfall. If we had gone south as we planned, we would have missed it. That didn't make me any less afraid, but it was some consolation.

I looked out at the street. It looked odd without my truck parked there. The truck towed it away after the EMTs left. I didn't get a chance to clean it out. I would have to go do that in a day or two.

I built a fire in the fireplace and we made s'mores by roasting marshmallows. We opened the curtains on the large windows in the living room so we could see the snowfall. It was a happy evening.

Again, I insisted that we all sleep in the same room. I asked the kids to make sure they locked the door again when they came back if they went out of the room. Then I said that

I didn't want them to leave the room. Not without one of us. Lucia thought I was being ridiculous. I wished so much that she could remember the duck man.

I woke in the night. I heard a sound. I thought it was in my dream. I raised my head so I could listen. I heard nothing. I needed to go to the bathroom.

I swung my legs over the side of the bed. The floor was cold. I put on my slippers and walked around the bed.

First, I saw that the bedroom door was open. That brought me fully awake. I switched on the light and saw that Daniela was not in her bag.

I might not have panicked right then but for the fact that cold air was wafting in through the open door. I took off running through the house.

The bathroom was empty. I called out Daniela's name as I sprinted down the hallway toward the living room.

"Daniela," I yelled when I entered the room. I stopped in the doorway.

A robust yell came from the creature who stood there with my daughter in his arms. It was the roar of a dragon, the bleating of a giant sheep, the scream of a goliath duck. The sound vibrated through me. I felt my insides shake and my bones threatened to crumble. Nausea overtook me and vomited all down the front of my pajamas. My legs wobbled and I had to grab the doorway to remain standing.

Its dark eyes stared into me. It had matted white hair all over its body. It had two sets of black horns like a goat. When it made its duck sound, great, sharp teeth shone from black gums and lips. Its head reached the ceiling of the living room. It had short, muscular legs and long feet that ended in hoof-like toes.

The nausea took me again and I doubled over. When I raised my head, the creature was darting into the kitchen. He still held Daniela in his arms.

"I'm playing with the no-man, Daddy," Daniela screamed as if she was going high on a swing at the playground. "He taking me to see Sanna Claus!" She did not fear this monster. I sure as hell did.

I bounded over to the fireplace and grabbed the poker. I cut into the kitchen and saw one w hite leg as it went out the back door. The storm door was wadded like aluminum foil and the wooden door stood open.

I ran out the back and into the alley with all the speed I could muster. The duck man was running down the alleyway at a speed that I could not believe.

I ran after it, brandishing my fireplace poker. At the end of the alley, it crossed the street. It cut between two houses and disappeared into the woods.

I followed. The monster and my daughter were out of sight by then. I ran deeper into the woods. The light dusting of snow was the only thing making sight possible in the dark night. I kept going.

I don't know how far I ran, but there was plenty more to go. They called this area the Kilderry. It was an area that was a tangled mess of rocks, trees and near-impenetrable growth. Homes out in the Kilderry were few and far between and the roads were as random as threads in a dollar bill.

I expected to come upon a road or a farmhouse eventually, but I didn't look for one. I followed anything that looked like a hoof print in the snow.

I saw when it ran. It got up on those three hoof-toes and that gave it some leg for running. Its stride was long and quick. I looked for those three-toed prints. In my madness, I saw them everywhere.

There have been several suns now. I'm not sure how many. I have not yet found a fence or a road or a home or my daughter. My legs pain me and I need water. I cannot rest, though. If I stop, she gets farther away.

I have yelled her name until my voice has turned to ash. I must find her soon. I must.

My tattered pajamas are no longer putting up a fight against the cold. I can't feel whether my slippers are still on my feet. Briar and cactus tear at my flesh. I'm certain there must be a creek around here. I will drink when I reach it. But I won't stop for more than a moment. Daniela is waiting for me. I must catch her and her captor, The 'No Man, The Duck Man.

10

SANTA BABY

DALE DRAKE

*T*ommy Stuckerman lay in the dark and listened to the sound of his sister weeping and smiled. They lived in a big house, what his father sometimes called a mini mansion. The children's rooms were side by side, his parent's room down the hall. This suited Tommy just fine. In the bright light of day, his little sister, Annabel, could stick close to their ever watchful nanny. Even at the tender age of four, she had already learned to give her big brother Tommy a very wide berth, but at night, in the dark, it was a different story. Tommy would lay awake for hours tossing and turning in his narrow bed as he fantasised about all the things he would do to his little sister.

When the hall light went out and his parents finally crawled into their bed, he would get up and sneak into his sister's room. That's when the fun would begin, and he always got away with it. He never left a mark and she had learned right from the start never to scream. The first time he had visited her, she had struggled and tried to yell for mummy and daddy but Tommy had clamped a large hand over her nose and mouth. He was seven and big for his age, no way she was getting away. Eventually, her struggles had become less frantic and her eyes had started to bulge, her skin turning an alarming shade of blue. Tommy had let her go then, but had promised if she ever screamed or told on him, he would put his hand back there again and never take it away.

What a thrill he had felt that first time, knowing he was in complete control, watching the fear in her eyes, feeling her helpless struggles beneath him, just like the time he had found the pigeon in the woods round the back of their house. Tommy had been playing ball while Annabel hid inside under the tender care of their nanny, Senorita Isabella. The Senorita did not like Tommy much and often sent him outside to play, even when the day was dark and overcast or even worse when his favourite T.V shows were on.

"Fucking bitch," Tommy had muttered, kicking his ball as hard as he could, perhaps imagining it was the Senorita's head as it sailed through the sky, bouncing past their perfectly manicured lawn before disappearing into the woods that surrounded their ten acre property. "Shit fire," Tommy said as he lumbered after the ball and into the shady treeline. Technically, Tommy was not allowed into the woods but the rules did not apply to him. The rules were for normal people and even at seven Tommy knew he was special.

The woods had been cool that day with stray rays of sunlight cutting through the leaf shrouded canopy, illuminating the forest floor. Tommy had spotted his ball right away. It had rolled down a small hillock and lay bobbing in a tiny trickling stream that weaved its way through the forest. Something splashed and fluttered beside his bobbing ball, a grey thing, and as Tommy drew closer, his ball all but forgotten, he saw that it was a small pigeon with a broken wing, all clawed up and bleeding.

He hurried over and fell to his knees, greedily scooping the struggling bird out of the cold water. Immediately, it began to peck at the back of his hand but Tommy did not mind a single bit. He was transfixed by the blood that coated the small bird's feathers and imagined he could see the panic in its little black beady eyes and feel the pounding of its fragile heart against the skin of his tight fist. There was a new sensation, now, and Tommy looked down at the bulge that had grown in the front of his pants, feeling a warm tingling sensation that was not entirely unpleasant.

Kneeling now, he slowly, almost reverently, put the bird back into the stream, holding it tighter, relishing the feeling of its feeble struggling as he slowly, oh so slowly, forced its head back under the freezing water.

He held it there for some time until its struggles started to become more feeble, before quickly dragging it back out. Thankfully, it was still alive, its beak opening and closing as if gasping for air. Tommy smiled a smile that would have sent his sister screaming from the room as he remembered the penknife in his jean's pocket. After that, things had become a little vague and misty. When Tommy had come to, all that was left of the bird was a red ruin in his hands, surrounded by a few sticky feathers and blood. There was blood everywhere, on his hands, between his fingers, even clotted under his fingernails. Guiltily, Tommy had looked around but there was no one near, nobody to see him scrape a shallow grave in the dirt or quickly wash his bloody hands in the freezing cold waters of the nearby stream.

Less than an hour later, he was back home, drinking milk and eating cookies in front of the T.V. When Annabel tottered in, a few moments later, he smiled at her, his best big brother smile, and asked her if she would like to go walking in the woods someday. The thought of all that had happened that day had excited Tommy all over again and he hopped out of bed, deciding to give Annabel a second helping for the night. It was Christmas Eve, after all, and she deserved a something special, a little Christmas treat, you might say.

He was just reaching for the door handle when something brushed against his toes, causing him to cry out and jump back in alarm. It was a note written on what looked like red card with silver glittery writing that seemed to glow in the dark. Almost, as if in a dream, Tommy reached down and picked it up, reading the words under his breath. The letter simply read, "Come down stairs. I have a gift for you. Love, Santa." As Tommy looked on in surprise, the letters slid off the page, showering his pyjama clad legs and naked feet in a cascading waterfall of glitter. Excited now, Tommy opened the door and hurriedly tip toed down the landing, trying desperately not to wake anyone. Santa was here and Tommy was not for sharing.

Taking the stairs two at a time, he ran down the marble staircase and into the main hall. There was a huge Christmas tree, reaching up towards the ornate ceiling, but it was the soft fire glow emanating from the sitting room to Tommy's right that drew his attention.

"Santa," he whispered, his whole body trembling with excitement. As he ran to the open doorway, skidding to a halt, his eyes widened as he looked on with amazement at the figure seated in his father's chair. It was Santa, bushy beard, red suit and all. "Santa," Tommy grinned. "It's really you."

"Sure is," Santa chuckled. "Come on over here, Tommy. You and I need to have a little chat." Tommy did as he was bid, kneeling with reverence at Santa's booted feet. From this position and even sitting down, Santa looked immensely tall. His face filled all of Tommy's vision as he looked down upon him with a toothy grin, a grin that turned into a grimace as if Santa had suddenly smelled something bad.

"You have been a bad boy, Tommy," he said, shaking his head sadly. "You have been a very bad boy indeed." With a sigh, he pulled an ancient looking parchment from between the brass buttons of his jolly red coat. "Do you know what this is, Tommy?" he said, brandishing the parchment like a club, causing a startled Tommy to recoil before the big man's anger. "This is the naughty list, Tommy, and your name is right at the top. That's a bad thing, Tommy, a very bad thing indeed. In fact, it's so bad that I am afraid you're going to have to come with me."

"With you?" Tommy said, trying to draw away but Santa's hand shot out, pinching the boy's arm cruelly. Tommy felt the power in the big man's hand and began to struggle and scream, shouting for his parents. But it was no good, Santa only shook his head, sadly.

"They're asleep, Tommy. Even that poor frightened child

you call a sister. They are all having the sweetest dreams. I sprinkled them with pixie dust," he chuckled, "an extra pinch for that poor sister of yours. Talking about your sister, I have an extra special gift for her and you," he said, shaking Tommy roughly, "are going to help me make it for her. You owe her that much, to be sure." Holding Tommy down, he reached behind his chair and, with a grunt, pulled out a large red sack. As Tommy watched on in horror, the bag began to pulse and undulate at Santa's touch. "Now," he said, dragging Tommy to his feet. "Now you get your present."

Quickly, deftly, Santa pulled open the sack and thrust a protesting Tommy's arm inside. Instantly, Tommy felt something slick and slimy grab his hand. For a second, there was a terrible flaring pain as something latched onto him, before he was brutally shoved away, tears streaming down his face as he held his now bleeding hand clutched tightly to his chest, his eyes bulging with terror as he watched the sack start to smoke and bulge. "Here it comes," Santa chuckled as the sack exploded in a blazing light of reds and greens. When the smoke disappeared, a boy stood in its place, a boy that looked exactly like Tommy, Thomas the Tank Engine pyjamas and all. The boy quickly looked around, his eyes passing over Tommy and lighting up as he recognised Santa.

"Is this my new home?" the boy said. "Oh say it is, Santa, please."

"It sure is, Tommy," he said, patting the boy's round cheek fondly. "Now you hurry up and get to bed and when you wake up, it will be like you have always been here."

"Sure," the new Tommy said, hurrying past the bleeding bad boy who recoiled at his passing.

"Oh and Tommy," Santa called after the prancing child. "You be extra nice to that sister of yours!"

"Of course," Tommy beamed. "I will love her just as much as a big brother can."

"That's a good lad," Santa said. "Now off to bed with you. It's Christmas Eve, after all, and all good children should be fast asleep." Tommy smiled, gave one last wave then disappeared upstairs. "Now," Santa said, grabbing up the naughty boy from across the room. "Time for us to go."

"Stop," the old Tommy screamed. "Please, I don't understand."

"What's to understand?" Santa said, thrusting the squirming boy into his sack. "You made the naughty list. You were going to grow up to be a very bad man, Tommy. You were going to hurt a lot of good people, starting with that poor sister of yours. But not now. Now you're coming with me."

"Where?" Tommy screamed, trying to fight his way out of the clinging sack. "Where are you taking me?"

"To Christmas Land, of course," Santa said, pushing him down. "There is a workbench there with your name on it. There you will make toys for all the good children of the world. You will make toys there, forever. But not to worry," he said, snapping closed the sack on Tommy's screaming face. "Every Christmas day you get to relax. Hell, sometimes we even take the chains off."

The End

11

THE CHRISTMAS CABIN FROM HELL

KEVIN J. KENNEDY

*C*hristmas can be a magical time of year, but it hadn't been that way for the Jones for quite some time. When their parents were alive, they would always make a point of getting together for at least a few days, but since both their parents had passed within a matter of days of each other, neither of the children had made an effort to spend time with the other. It wasn't a case of a family feud or ill will. They were both too busy with their careers and each year just seemed to pass with one or the other or both being too busy for a reunion. That is until this year. Both had been planning it since autumn. They made sure they had arranged time off work and as the days passed by, they both became more excited about reigniting a family tradition. Colin had rented them a log cabin in the woods and sent pictures to Susan. She got back to him immediately when they popped up in her work email account. She thought it looked wonderful and the scenery was beautiful. She thought it would look even better if they were to get snow this Christmas.

The weeks passed by slowly with the siblings eager to see each other again. They spoke more over email than they had over the last few years and even had a few happy telephone conversations. They discussed what each of them would need to bring and wrote lists so nothing would be forgotten. Only a few days before they were due to head out to the cabin, the snow started to fall. You could never tell if you would get snow in Scotland for Christmas. The weather was generally cold but often the snow would start to fall in February and into March and that would be it for the year. The seasons often seemed to be a little out of sync.

The siblings had a last phone call on Thursday evening. Colin planned to drive out to the cabin and arrive on Friday evening and Susan would leave early Saturday morning and arrive around lunch time. They had added extra time to the drive for the weather.

When Colin arrived at the cabin, it looked a little more run down than the pictures had shown from the outside, but they had probably been taken a while ago. He needn't have worried though. It was immaculate inside. It looked even bigger from the inside than it did outside. There was no dust anywhere and the furniture all looked relatively modern. The most important part, though, was the large fireplace that had been built into the cabin. Although the cabin was made of wood, the fireplace was made of brick. It was just like the one that his parents had in their house. When he saw it in the brochure, he knew this was the place where he would bring Susan for their first Christmas back together.

After bringing his luggage in from the car, he hung his jacket over the back of one of the wooden chairs that sat at the dining table and began to try and build a fire. He had never had to do it at his parents'. Any time he arrived; the fire was already roaring. It didn't take all that much trying. The wood had been stored inside so it was bone dry and there was some kindling and paper to help get things going. As it got under way, he sat back in one of the comfy chairs that were positioned at either side of the fireplace and watched. It didn't take long before his mind wandered, and he fell asleep. His dreams brought back wonderful old memories of better times.

When Colin woke up, everything was dark. He checked his watch, and it was three in the morning. He had slept for hours. He decided to leave unpacking for the morning. Before heading off to bed, he decided he would need to pour himself a glass of malt. It was a tradition here carried out every night to help him get to sleep. The log fire had sent him to slumberland earlier, but he now worried he wouldn't get back to sleep in his bedroom. As he went to his holdall and removed a bottle of Aberlour A'bunadh, he realised the fire was beginning to die. He found a glass from the sideboard and half-filled it. He didn't consider himself a big drinker, but he did like a large whiskey before bed. The next thing he knew, he had added a few logs to the fire and was back in his chair, or at least the chair he now considered his. He doubted Susan would fuss over it. She was always easily pleased. Before long, the glass of malt was downed, and Colin fell back into a deep sleep.

The following morning, there was a loud, continuous

chapping at the door. Colin woke groggily and realised he had once again fallen asleep in front of the fire. He got up and walked over to the door, rubbing the sleep from his eyes. He pulled the door open and there stood his sister.

"Susan, wow, hi. How did you get here so early?"

"So early? I t's eleven- thirty. I said I would be here around twelve, but I made good time. Are you okay?"

"Um, yeh. I guess I overslept. I planned to unpack and tidy up a little. It's that log fire, it's just too cosy, " Colin said and laughed.

He reached out and lifted her suitcase off the cabin deck.

"I see you still overpack. We are only here for a few days and no one is going to see you apart from me."

"How do you know that all that extra weight isn't your Christmas present?" Susan said, smirking.

"Because I know you too well."

Susan punched Colin on the arm and started to take off her woolly hat and scarf.

"It's really beautiful out here. I'm glad the snow was off for the drive, but this place looks like it should be on a Christmas card."

"Yeh, it's truly stunning. Once we get you settled, we could go a- wander if you've brought decent boots to wade through the snow."

"You've felt the weight of my case. What do you think?"

"Point taken, you have it covered. We better not wander too far though. I don't think there will be much help out here if we get lost."

"What bedroom am I in? I'll get ready. "

"Either. I fell asleep in the armchair last night. I never made it to bed."

"My god, you must have been comfy."

There was a bedroom door at either end of the fireplace. Susan chose the one on the left and carried her suitcase in. She switched on the light, told Colin she wouldn't be long and closed the door.

Colin felt a little worse for wear. He felt dehydrated from the whiskey and no doubt sleeping so close to the fire. He decided to have a little more of the Aberlour. Not that his sister would probably bother other than the fact it was early in the day, but he poured some into the glass from the night before and swallowed it back quickly. He decided it wasn't worth showering and changing so he got his wellies from the door. He had driven up wearing them and kicked them off when he entered. It didn't take long before Susan was ready. Just as they were about to leave, there was a thud against the door, then another a second later against the wall of the cabin. A few seconds after, there were three or four thuds in quick succession. Colin ran over to the window to see what was going on. There was no one standing at their door and there didn't seem to be anyone outside. Everything was white apart from the two cars. The only thing that was completely out of place was the three snowmen that had appeared outside.

"Um, sis. You didn't happen to build a few snowmen before you came into the cabin this morning, did you?"

"Snowmen, what are you talking about?" Susan said, pushing in next to Colin at the window. "Wow, where did they come from?"

Susan knew she hadn't been in the cabin long and Colin didn't think she would have stood outside building the snowmen as a joke.

"Do you think some local kids came by and built them?" Susan asked Colin.

"I don't think there are any local kids. I can't see any footsteps around them, either."

Colin could feel the malt sinking into his system. It brought warmth to his stomach. He felt confident and brave.

"I'll go out and have a look around, " Colin said.

"What about the bangs against the cabin? "

"Probably just snow falling off the roof."

"And banging the cabin door and wall?" Susan said, doubtful.

"It'll be okay. Let me go and check."

With that, Colin pulled open the door and stepped outside. As he did a flurry of snowballs hit him at once. One was right in the face and some of the ice went in his eyes. He staggered backwards and felt Susan put her arms around him and pull him inside. He heard the door slam before he managed to get his eyes open again. Everything was blurry.

"Oh my god, are you okay?" Susan asked, panicking.

"I'm fine. It was just a few snowballs. Should have expected it. You must be right. There must be kids around."

"Colin, those weren't kids. I stayed at the window so I could watch you. The snowmen threw the snowballs."

"What do you mean the snowmen through them? The kids will be hiding behind them. Probably built them for that exact purpose."

"No, honestly, as you pulled open the door, I watched as

they pulled back their arms and threw them at you. Come here and see. They are moving."

Susan sounded more panicked than Colin ever heard her. She was normally the rational one. His eyes were clearing, although they still stung, but he made his way to his feet and back to the window. It was true enough; the snowmen were moving. All three looked perfectly formed. More like snowmen off a postcard rather than the kind you build yourself. They had large, perfectly round bottom halves to their bodies, slightly smaller midsections and then heads that were a little smaller than the midsections. Each of them was identical. The heads looked more like jack o' lanterns than they did snowmen heads, but it was clear they were made of snow.

"This doesn't make any sense. They weren't there when you arrived, were they?" Colin asked .

"No, if they were, I would have thought you made them, and I would have mentioned them. I've barely been here twenty minutes, though. How could someone build them so quickly?"

"I don't think they did, Susan. I mean, snowmen don't move by themselves, or at all for that matter. Not unless they are mechanical ones that you see at fayres or in store windows. There are no wires coming from them that I can see."

Just as Colin stopped talking, there was another barrage of snowballs that hit the cabin.

"What the fuck?"

Colin had never heard Susan swear before.

"Listen. We will be okay. I mean, they are only snowmen. What can they really do?"

"Well, they seemed to manage to hurt you pretty quickly."

"We just need to wrap up in our best snow clothes and make a break for the cars. We will take both sets of keys but let's go for your car, as it's a little closer."

"Are you crazy? We would need to run right past them to get to the cars."

"We will go the long way round. They are over to the left, so let's go wide around the snowman on the furthest left."

"I think this is a bad idea."

"The other option is to sit and get drunk and try and forget about it. They don't seem to be getting any closer to the cabin."

"No, let's try. Getting drunk isn't going to achieve anything."

"Okay, let's get into our gear."

Ten minutes later, brother and sister were as wrapped up as they could be. Best snow jackets, and waterproof trousers tucked into their wellies. Two pairs of socks, scarves and woolie hats.

"It's a pity we don't have snow goggles, " Colin said, remembering how the snowball felt. He knew it had been more ice than snow, but he hadn't wanted to worry Susan. "Ready?"

"As I'll ever be."

Colin rubbed Susan's shoulder, which she could barely feel through the puffy winter jacket, but it was the closest they had been in years.

"We will be okay, go wide and stay to my left and, hopefully, I will get the brunt of whatever they throw, " Colin said.

The minute the door was opened, the ice balls started to

fly. Brother and sister kept their heads down and made a run for it. They had to go quite far over to the left of the cabin before they made way to the cars, and neither of them were very fit. The snowmen kept up the assault and most of it hit Colin when he heard a scream and realised that Susan stopped running. He jogged back to her wondering if she had sprained an ankle, but she just stood there with her mouth wide. More ice balls hit Colin on the back as he tried to shield her.

"Come on, we need to get out of here, " he said, giving her a gentle shake.

She raised her arm and pointed ahead. Colin turned swiftly, still trying to keep his head forward and prevent another ice ball in the eyes. He almost fainted at what he saw. Right in front of the cars stood three snow leopards. Not only was that strange in the fact that they weren't native to Scotland, but on the back of each rode what could only be described as an elf. Not the *Lord of the Rings* kind, either. The Elf on a Shelf type. They were probably about four feet tall and had menacing, goblin-like faces. Although no snow fell on Colin or Susan, snow seemed to sweep around the elves and snow leopards. It was as if they had their own small weather cycle surrounding them.

"That can not be real!" Colin exclaimed.

Susan still said nothing. A particularly large and solid ice ball hit Colin on the head and woke him up a bit. He grabbed Susan by her gloved hand and began to drag her back to the cabin. Although she didn't resist, she moved slowly as if in some sort of trance. Fear had taken over and she zoned out, but they managed to make their way back, get inside and get the door slammed shut and locked before anything happened to them. Both collapsed on the floor with their backs to the door. The snowmen continued to throw their snow and ice balls.

As the assault on the door stopped, neither noticed. Colin was in absolute wonderment as to what was going on and Susan was still staring into space on the brink of a break-down. Colin realised they needed to look out of the windows and see what the hell was going on. First, he would need to get Susan warm and comfy. He helped lift her from the floor and she let him lead her to the comfy chair he had sat in the night before. He eased her into it and started the fire. As soon as the fire was lit, he poured her a large malt and helped guide it to her lips. Once she took a sip, he put the bottle to his lips and took several large gulps. He sat it down on one of the tables that sat between the comfy chairs and slowly creeped back to the window.

When Colin peered out, the snowmen were exactly where they had been, but their crooked, pumpkin-like smiles looked even more menacing. More worryingly was the fact that the snowcats with the elves on their backs had drawn forward and were now closer to the cabin than the snowmen.

"What the fuck? This is insane, " Colin said to himself. He could feel the glow from the malt but it did nothing to calm his nerves. Deciding they needed to do something, he ran to his bag and pulled out his mobile phone. He would call the police, but he would lie and say someone was breaking in. They would never believe the truth. He put his code into the phone to unlock it and a *HO HO HO!* f lashed up on the screen. He tried pressing the screen and the few buttons around the body of the phone and nothing happened. The *HO HO HO!* stayed where it was. He ran over to Susan.

"Susan, give me your phone."

Almost as if on auto pilot, she reached into her jacket pocket and pulled it out while she stared into space and sipped at the malt. Colin quickly swiped her screen to get the same message. *HO HO HO!*

"This can't be happening."

Colin knew the cabin had no landline. He rushed back to the window and looked outside again. Three snowmen and three snow leopards with elves riding them. Two of the snow leopards were almost at the side of the cabin while the rest of the nightmares from hell had the front covered. Colin decided to check the rooms and see if there was another way out. He rushed into Susan's room first, as the door was open. There was only one window and it faced the side of the cabin. He knew if they tried to escape that way, the snow cats would be on them. There was no sky light or any other way of leaving the cabin. He checked the other room, and it was the same, except everything was mirrored. Lastly, he went into the toilet, but it had a tiny little window that neither of them would have been able to squeeze their way out of. He rushed back into the main room and over to Susan.

"Sis, there is no way out of here apart from the front door or the side windows. We can either try and wait this out, or we can make a break for it. Whatever way we go, I think we are going to need to fight. Even if we go out the side windows, we will still need to go for the cars since there is nothing back there but woods."

Susan's eyes registered for the first time since we got back into the house.

"Why is this happening to us? Do you think we are being punished?"

"No, I don't. What would we be being punished for?"

"I don't know. It just doesn't seem real."

"No, it doesn't, but nonetheless, here we are. We have been through a lot and we can get through this… but we are going to have to fight. You with me?"

Susan looked at the glass of malt. She stared at it for a few seconds and Colin worried she was going back into a catatonic state, then she put it to her lips, flung her head back and downed what was left in the glass.

"Fuck it. Let's get out of this shit hole. We should have stayed in the city. Fuckin' cabin in the woods bullshit!"

Colin once again noticed her use of bad language. While it was out of character, so would be fighting a pack of snowmen, snow leopards and elves. While even thinking it seemed crazy, he believed his own eyes and knew Susan had seen them, too.

"Let's get some weapons, " Colin said as Susan rose from her chair. She had a much more determined look on her face now.

They each hunted around the cabin, but there wasn't a whole lot to use. They got a few big knives out of the small, makeshift kitchen that the cabin had, but other than that, they couldn't find anything weapon-like.

"Sis, before we go out here. Let's have one more drink, a cheers to family. I'm glad Mum and Dad aren't here to see this. If they were alive, we would be at their house anyway, but they are not. It's just us now, and we need to stick together. If anything happens to me, I want you to make sure you get into one of those cars and get out of here."

Colin held out his set of keys.

"No arguing, come on, take them."

Susan reluctantly took the keys.

"I don't want to leave without you.

"I know, but if only one of us makes it, it has to be you. Promise?"

"I promise, " Susan said as a tear rolled down her cheek.

"Come on, none of that now. We are getting ready for battle, " Colin said, forcing the best cheeky smile he could onto his face.

"You're right. Let's show these fuckheads that you don't mess with the Jonese s."

Colin poured more malt into each glass and threw a few extra logs with some paper onto the fire to get a good heat into their bones before they headed outside. As the fire kicked up he raised his glass.

"To family. Those here and those who are no longer with us. Mum and Dad, send us some luck. Love you guys."

And with that, brother and sister clinked glasses and took a large drink each. For the next few minutes they both sipped at their drinks while staring into the roaring fire.

"That's it!" Susan shouted.

Colin almost spilled what remained of his drink all over himself.

"We have weapons. Anything we can turn into a torch is a weapon, surely. The snowmen should melt, but that aside, I don't think there is anything alive that can't be killed with fire."

Colin stared at her for a few seconds. "You are a genius, sis."

He jumped up and ran to the small closet. It had a mop and a broom. Both of those would work. He gave them to Susan, who started to wrap the tops of them with some bandages she pulled from her bag. That woman carried everything you might need. When Colin couldn't find anything else they could use, he upturned a table and broke two of the legs off it. Susan wrapped those, too. Once they had their homemade torches ready, they each drank what was left in their glasses and poured the remainder of the bottle over the bandaged end of the torches. Before lighting them, they slipped the few knives into their pockets, being careful to angle them so they wouldn't cut themselves, and then picked up two torches each. They nodded at each other and then put the tops of the torches into the fire. They lit quickly.

"Okay, I'm going out the door first. I want you to try and stay behind me as much as possible and same plan as last time, we swing out to the left."

Colin had a little difficulty opening the door with the torch in his hand, but he managed. The second he stepped outside, the snowmen started to fire the ice balls again. They seemed even larger and more solid now. He looked over his shoulder to make sure Susan was following and started making his way to the left. It was scary enough when it had just been the snowmen, but now the snow leopards marched towards them in sync with the evil Christmas elves on top of them. He could see now that the elves had large fangs.

"Come on, keep moving, " he said over his shoulder.

"Right behind you."

As they spoke, the leopards moved even closer. Susan managed to keep Colin between her and the large cats.

"When they get close enough to me, I want you to run for the car. I'll hold them off. You need to get the car open. Get in and lock your side, but get ready to open a door for me."

"But Colin..."

"SUSAN! We agreed to this already!"

"Okay. Please be careful."

"I will. Now get ready. Keep your torches until you get to the car."

Within seconds, the devil cats made a semi-circle around Colin.

"NOW!" he shouted as Susan broke off in a run. One of the cats nearest to her went to chase after her but Colin dove forward and stuck his torch right into its side. The cat let out an almighty roar. The elf on top was thrown from its back. Unlike a real cat, the snow leopard began to melt. Although it seemed entirely solid in form, it looked like it was turning to mushy snow. It also doused Colin's torch, so he used it to smash the elf in the head. It knocked the elf onto its back as another cat tried to attack him from the side. Once again, he jabbed the cat with his torch, and once again, the cat roared and fell over before starting to melt. There was now only one elf left on a cat and two on the ground. Colin held onto his second doused torch and began swinging at the elves. He hit the one that was still standing square in the temple. It collapsed where it stood but just as he did it, the final snow leopard pounced and landed on him, its two massive paws pinning him to the ground. The elf sat atop it cackled.

"Thought you would escape us, did you?" it said in a shrill, gargled voice.

Just as Colin was waiting to have his head ripped from his shoulders, he remembered the knife in his pocket. He quickly pulled it out and buried it in the cat, but the cat barely moved. It seemed to have no effect on it. It seemed that only fire would work against these demons.

Just as Colin was hoping that his death was a quick one, he heard another shrill scream. This one came from his sister, though. Even from his vantage point under the large predator, he could see his sister running at pace towards it. She had both torches held high. He could see the car door lying open. She had made it to the car but had come back for him. He wasn't sure whether to be happy or cry. As her feet got closer, his view became more obscured, but she thrust one of her torches at the cat and the other at its rider. The cat quickly began to melt and as it did, the elf rider melted through it, squealing in flames. Colin rolled to the side, but some of the flames caught his jacket. He rolled more in the snow to extinguish the fire and as soon as it was out, got up onto all fours to see where his sister was.

Only one of the elves was back on its feet and she was beating it with the extinguished torch. Wondering if the knife would work on the elves, Colin scooped his up as he ran towards them and buried it in the elf's back. He wrapped his arm around its neck and pulled it off its feet. Once it was on the ground, him and Susan stamped furiously on its head until there was nothing left but a pile of mush. They both turned to see the last elf still passed out. Snow and ice balls continued to rain down on them the whole time but neither of them barely noticed now. As they walked towards the last elf, Susan pulled two knives from her pockets and handed one to Colin. They began stabbing the elf in a frenzy and by the time they were done, it must have had over a hundred holes in it and Colin almost severed its head from its spine.

The battle took it out of both of them and they could barely breathe.

"Go get the car sis and pull it closer to the cabin. I've got something to do."

"What about the snowmen?" Susan asked as Colin jumped into the passenger seat and she began to reverse.

"The fire from the cabin will melt them. It's time we left this place."

As Susan drove down the road, wondering what the hell just happened, and Colin started out the window, they were both covered in cuts and bruises, not to mention the large claw marks that had cut into Colin's shoulders.

It was quiet for a while. Both in shock but both also amazed that they survived the ordeal, when Colin finally broke the ice.

"Sis, how about we just have Christmas at my house?"

"That sounds like a plan. I think I may need another few glasses of malt, though."

"I think that can be arranged. Want me to drive the rest of the way?"

"No, you get some rest. You took the worst of it. I'll patch you up when we get home."

"Thanks, sis, you are the best. Merry Christmas.

"Merry Christmas to you too, little bro."

Colin quickly faded off to sleep and Susan drove the rest of the way. She didn't want to wake him. It took them both a while to recover from their ordeal, but they never spent another Christmas apart.

The End

ACKNOWLEDGMENTS

I would like to take a moment to give an awesome standing ovation to our talented cover artist, Dean Samed. He has created a cover that reflects the spirit of true Chistmas horrors.

Dean can be found at:

https://www.facebook.com/deansamed

Don't forget to pick up your Fractured Mind Publishing merchandise on Amazon. With styles ranging from t-shirts to hoodies, we have something for men, women, and youth.

Some Examples

FMP Baseball Tee

FMP T-shirt

www.ingramcontent.com/pod-product-compliance
Lightning Source LLC
Chambersburg PA
CBHW051507260626
47162CB00008B/2865